WE HAD
TO REMOVE
THIS POST

Hanna Bervoets is one of the most acclaimed Dutch writers of her generation. She is the author of seven novels in her home country of the Netherlands, and she has also written screenplays, plays, short stories and essays. She is the recipient of many literary awards, including the prestigious Frans Kellendonk Prize for her entire body of work. She was a resident at Art Omi: Writers at Ledig House, New York, and currently works and lives in Amsterdam with her girlfriend and two guinea pigs. *We Had To Remove This Post* has been translated into thirteen languages and is her first book to be translated into English.

WE HAD TO REMOVE THIS POST

Hanna Bervoets

Translated by Emma Rault

PICADOR

First published 2022 by HarperCollins

First published in the UK 2022 by Picador
an imprint of Pan Macmillan
The Smithson, 6 Briset Street, London EC1M 5NR
EU representative: Macmillan Publishers Ireland Ltd, 1st Floor,
The Liffey Trust Centre, 117–126 Sheriff Street Upper,
Dublin 1, D01 YC43
Associated companies throughout the world
www.panmacmillan.com

ISBN 978-1-5290-8723-9

Copyright © Hanna Bervoets 2021
Translation copyright © Emma Rault 2022

The right of Hanna Bervoets to be identified as the
author of this work has been asserted by her in accordance
with the Copyright, Designs and Patents Act 1988.

Originally published as *Wat wij zagen* in the Netherlands in 2021
by Stichting Collectieve Propaganda van het Nederlandse Boek.

All rights reserved. No part of this publication may be reproduced,
stored in a retrieval system, or transmitted, in any form, or by any means
(electronic, mechanical, photocopying, recording or otherwise)
without the prior written permission of the publisher.

Pan Macmillan does not have any control over, or any responsibility for,
any author or third-party websites referred to in or on this book.

1 3 5 7 9 8 6 4 2

A CIP catalogue record for this book is available from the British Library.

Typeset by Palimpsest Book Production Ltd, Falkirk, Stirlingshire
Printed and bound by CPI Group (UK) Ltd, Croydon, CR0 4YY

This book is sold subject to the condition that it shall not, by way of
trade or otherwise, be lent, hired out, or otherwise circulated without
the publisher's prior consent in any form of binding or cover other than
that in which it is published and without a similar condition including
this condition being imposed on the subsequent purchaser.

Visit **www.picador.com** to read more about all our books
and to buy them. You will also find features, author interviews and
news of any author events, and you can sign up for e-newsletters
so that you're always first to hear about our new releases.

WE HAD
TO REMOVE
THIS POST

/ / /

So what kinds of things did you see?

It's crazy how often people still ask me that, even though it's been sixteen months since I left Hexa. People just won't stop trying, and if my answer doesn't live up to their expectations—too vague, not shocking enough—they simply repeat the question, putting it slightly differently. "But what's the *worst* thing you ever saw?" Gregory, my new colleague at the museum, asks me.

"So what exactly are we talking about here?" That's

Leabharlanna Poiblí Chathair Baile Átha Cliath
Dublin City Public Libraries

my Aunt Meredith, who for years I would only see on the anniversary of Mom's death, but who has suddenly gotten into the habit of calling me on the first Sunday of every month to ask how I'm doing, and oh yeah, what exactly it was that I saw.

"Why don't you choose one video, one image, or one post that really affected you." And there's Dr. Ana. "Tell me what you thought and felt at the time. Go ahead and make it into an image in your head . . . Yes, a mental image of yourself sitting there and seeing that upsetting image" —and then she pulls out some sort of rod with a light flashing back and forth inside of it.

And now you've joined in too, Mr. Stitic. You call me almost every day now. "Please get in touch when you have a moment, Ms. Kayleigh." Do you even realize that Kayleigh is my first name? You don't, do you? Of course you got a hold of my details from my former colleagues, who don't know my last name, and now you're asking me: "So, Ms. Kayleigh, what kinds of things did you see?"

People act like it's a perfectly normal question, but how normal *is* a question when you're expecting the answer to be gruesome? And it's not like any of those people are asking out of concern for my well-being. Maybe that's not so strange—maybe questions don't stem from interest in the other person so much as curiosity about the lives we might have led ("Gosh, Mr. Stitic, civil law . . . what's that like?"), but with Gregory and Aunt Meredith, and even with Dr. Ana, I can't help but suspect a certain amount of lurid fascination, an urge that compels them to ask but that can never be fully satisfied.

I saw a livestream of a girl sticking a much-too-dull pocketknife into her own arm—she really had to jam it in there before a decent amount of blood would come out. I saw a man kicking his German shepherd so hard that the poor animal slammed into the fridge, whimpering. I saw kids daring each other to eat dangerously large amounts of cinnamon in one go. I saw people singing Hitler's praises to their neighbors, colleagues, and vague acquaintances, publicly, unabashedly, out there for potential partners and employers to see: "Hitler should have finished what he started" below a picture of a group of immigrants crammed into a small boat.

But those are all cop-out examples—you know that, don't you? Those things have all been in the papers, culled from accounts by other former moderators, though that doesn't mean I didn't encounter them too: the abused dogs, the Nazi salutes—and the girl with the knives is a classic, there are thousands of them, one on every street, or at least that's how I picture it: That house where the bathroom light is still on at night, that's where she's sitting alone on the cold, hard floor. But that's not what people want to hear. They want me to give them something new, things they'd never dare look at, things that are far beyond their imagination, which is why Gregory asks, "But what's the *worst* thing you ever saw?" rather than "How is that girl doing now? Were you able to help her, by any chance?" God no, people have no idea what my previous job actually entailed, and that's partly your fault, Mr. Stitic. After all the news about the lawsuit you're filing on behalf of my former colleagues, people believe that we all sat there in front of our screens like zombies, that we didn't know what we were doing, had no idea what we'd gotten ourselves into, that out of the blue we were bombarded with thousands of sickening images that short-circuited the synapses in our brains almost instantly— well, it wasn't like that. At least not entirely, and not for everyone.

I knew what I was getting myself into. I knew what I was doing, and I was pretty damn good at it. I still remember all the rules from back then and I still apply them sometimes, it happens automatically, an occupational hazard—whether it's TV shows, video clips, or just things I see in my everyday life. That woman getting knocked off her scooter—can you put that up online? Not if you can see blood. If the situation is clearly comical, then yes. If there's sadism involved, no. If what's being shown serves an educational purpose, yes, and *ding ding ding,* we have a winner, because that exit to the museum parking lot is a hot mess. "They really need to fix that," as long as I put that in the caption, it's allowed—see, that's the kind of thing I'm thinking about as I tear off four tickets for a visitor. And no, it's not always pleasant having those rules rattling around in my head, but you know what? Part of me is still proud of how well I knew the guidelines. That's just not what you want to hear, is it?

I haven't replied to any of your emails. I haven't returned any of your calls, either—I thought you would have gotten the message by now. I don't want to talk to you. I don't want to join the other plaintiffs. *I don't want to be involved in your lawsuit.* But you just keep calling and calling, and today I received your second letter (very elegant handwriting you have, Mr. Stitic).

It's not that I don't understand. You're a lawyer, it's

your job to keep insisting, and you're pretty well versed in the art of persuasion—don't think I haven't noticed how your tone has gotten a little chummier with each message. You know I'm listening, you know I'm getting used to the sound of your voice, so you've stopped calling me "Ms. Kayleigh" and are suddenly talking about "the prospect of a decent sum of money," and to be honest I think it's pretty creepy that you know how badly I could use a decent sum of money. I'm sure my former colleagues have told you about my debts, and I wonder how that comports with the applicable privacy regulations, but hey, I'm sure you know that better than me.

Two more years at the museum and I will have paid it all off. That is, if I work overtime during the holidays, when the pay's better, so here's hoping I get shifts on Easter and Boxing Day too, because no, there's no way I'm going to join in with this thing, though I understand why my former colleagues have.

I read that Robert sleeps with his taser these days, afraid that terrorists will come and kidnap him at night (the names in that newspaper article had been changed, but "Timothy" can only be Robert, I'm sure of it). That "Nataly" can't handle loud noises, bright lights, or sudden movement in her peripheral vision (there were a bunch of people who struggled with that, so I'm not sure who Nataly is). I know that many of my former colleagues flinch when someone comes up behind them in the supermarket, that they lie in bed until after dark and then stay up till it's light—too exhausted to start a new job, they see things, day and night, the same things I don't like to talk about either, and I'm sorry to say that some of those symptoms aren't exactly foreign to me. And yes, just like many of my former colleagues, I left Hexa of my own accord— so again, I understand why you've come knocking on my door.

But for you to understand why I won't be taking you up on your offer, there's something you need to know about me first. The images that keep me up at night, Mr. Stitic, aren't the gruesome pictures of bleeding teenagers, or the videos of stabbings or decapitations. No, what keeps me awake are images of Sigrid, my dearest former colleague. Sigrid held up against a wall, limp and gasping for air—those are the images that *I* would like to forget.

So I'm writing to you with a proposal. See it as a deal— a settlement. I'll tell you about my months at Hexa, about my duties, the rules, the famously deplorable working conditions—things, in short, that are sure to interest you.

And then I will explain why I left Hexa. I've never told

anyone that, but I will be honest, completely honest. Once you know, you will understand why I won't become one of your clients, Mr. Stitic—in fact, you probably won't even want to help me anymore.

All I want in return is for you to keep quiet and leave me alone for good. No emails, no phone calls, no showing up at my door. If my former colleagues ask about me, just tell them I moved abroad, make something up, I'm sure you won't have any trouble with that.

Be aware, however, that this letter is not an official testimony. I won't be mentioning the name of the defendant at any point—you know that doing so would be a violation of my contract, I've sought advice on the subject, I'm aware of my legal position—so once again: I'm not accusing anyone of anything. I'm only telling you my story, just this once.

/ / /

There were nineteen people in the October cohort. Before we started we all attended a mandatory training, and
what I remember most from that week is Alice, a blond
woman on crutches who I'd guess was at least thirty years
older than most of us. During a cigarette break, Alice said
that before this she'd been a social worker. I remember
thinking, What is someone like that doing here? (Later,
Sigrid told me that's exactly what she'd thought about *me:*
What on earth is that Kayleigh doing here? She'd noticed

me right away, she said, she thought I was intriguing, with my short hair and wrinkled NOFX T-shirt, I looked like I didn't care what anyone else thought about me and she found that extremely sexy.) Whenever I peered past my computer screen that week, I'd look at Alice, who always seemed to be completely absorbed in her work, her crutches leaning at an angle against her desk. In the breaks I usually went up to her. She was old enough to be my mother, and I felt attracted to her in a strange, not necessarily erotic way. Alice didn't say much—she was hard to read—but on day three I heard her say that she thought people who chewed gum were gross ("It's the texture, like a booger in someone's mouth") and I immediately swallowed my Stimorol.

I didn't talk to anyone else from our cohort. I wasn't here to make friends, I told myself—after all, wasn't that how things had gone south at my last job? Thanks to my having been so, shall we say, sociable, I was now stuck with a blocked credit card. The main reason I'd applied for a job at Hexa was because their hourly rate was twenty percent higher than at the call center I was working in at the time.

The ad hadn't said much else—apart from a salary indication, it only offered a succinct job description: Hexa was looking for "quality assurance workers"—I had to look up what that meant, but for twenty percent more pay I would have been happy to pick up garbage. At the interview, which wasn't particularly in-depth, I was told that Hexa was just a subcontractor. In actuality, I would be "evaluating content" for a large and powerful tech company whose name, they told me before I'd so much as touched a contract, I was not ever, under any circumstances, allowed to mention. I soon learned that this platform—your defendant—determined all of our rules, working hours, and guidelines. And all of the posts, images, and videos we'd be reviewing had been reported as "offensive" by users or bots on this specific platform and its subsidiaries. On the first day of our weeklong training, we, the October cohort, bright-eyed, bushy-tailed, and eager to please, did our very best not to mention this actual employer, until we discovered that our trainers, a guy and a girl who, they told us, had started out as moderators themselves—thereby suggesting, whether they meant to or not, that this kind of ascent was within the realm of possibility for all of us (a motivating prospect that I think compelled some of the people from our cohort to stay with Hexa longer than was good for them)—both used the name of the platform freely. *The platform feels this,* they said, *The platform allows that*, and we soon began to understand that we were mainly supposed to maintain secrecy from the outside world. Here, in the office tower where Hexa was based, safely tucked away in a business park with its own bus stop, we were among equals, brethren in a secret society. This training was an initiation, a hazing ritual to make sure we were fit for admission. At least, that's what I believed back then.

We were given two manuals that first day, one with the terms and conditions of the platform and one with the guidelines for moderators. We didn't know at the time that those guidelines changed constantly and that the tome we received was already outdated when it was put into our hands. We weren't allowed to take the manuals home with us, so we learned by doing. On the first day of training, a series of text-only posts appeared on our screens, and then, from day three, photos, videos, and livestreams. Each time, the question was: Is it okay to leave this up on the platform? And if not, *why* not? That last part was the trickiest. The platform doesn't allow people to post things like "All Muslims are terrorists," because Muslims are a PC, a "protected category," just like women, gay people, and, believe it or not, Mr. Stitic, heterosexuals. "All terrorists are Muslims," on the other hand, *is* allowed, because terrorists are not a PC and besides, *Muslim* isn't an offensive term. A video of someone flinging their cat out the window is only allowed if cruelty is not a motive; a photo of someone flinging their cat out the window is always allowed; a video of people kissing in bed is allowed as long as we don't see any genitalia or female nipples; male nipples are permitted at all times. A hand-drawn penis in a vagina is allowed; digital drawings of vulvas are not allowed; a naked child can only be shown if the image pertains to a news story, unless it's about the Holocaust; pictures of underage Holocaust victims with no clothes on are forbidden. A picture of a gun meets the standards, but not if the gun is being offered for sale. Death threats against a pedophile are allowed; death threats against a politician are not; a video of a religious zealot blowing themselves up in a daycare center should be removed, on the grounds that it's terrorist propaganda, not because it depicts violence or child abuse. If we selected the wrong category, our assessment was considered incorrect, regardless of whether or not the post needed to be taken down. We reviewed two hundred posts a day that first week (yes, once we'd been hired we would have to do a fair amount more than that), and at the end of each day we were shown our accuracy scores. Hexa aimed for an accuracy score of 97 percent, and initially I was frustrated when

I didn't get above 85. Until I started sneaking peeks at Kyo's screen. Kyo, who may have been ten years younger than me—the ballpoint doodles on his backpack told me he'd probably only just finished high school—often sat next to me, and his score was never over 75 percent, which was somewhat encouraging. But when Alice told me at the bus stop on day four that she'd correctly evaluated a whopping 98 percent of her "tickets," I decided to lay off the beer that night to see if I'd do any better the next day.

I don't know how Sigrid fared during those first few days. If you asked me when I truly noticed her for the first time, I would say it was on the last day of our training, during our exam. It was a rather strange exercise, I thought, a kind of oral exam, but in front of the entire cohort. One by one we were called up to the front of the room. We'd all be shown a video or an image and then the person whose turn it was had to say why it did or did not comply with the guidelines. Alice was shown footage of a baby that was put down on a dirt road by a grown woman and then stoned by two boys. She stood there in her over-size denim jacket, leaning on one crutch, cool as a cucumber, and passed with flying colors: "Child abuse, subcategory violent death, maybe—however, no glorification in the caption, so leave it up, but flag it as alarming." Sigrid did well too, but what struck me more than anything was the way she stood there. Whereas the others all spoke with a slightly questioning inflection but didn't otherwise sound that different from usual, Sigrid assumed a confident pose, surveying us with clasped hands like a butler welcoming his master's guests. "What we have here," she said, loudly and with clear enunciation, "is a case of sexual content, with a female nipple occurring at the three-minutes-and-four-seconds mark. The areola is clearly visible, which means this post must be removed on account of containing female nudity, although the caption—'I hope it hurts'—implies there is also sadism involved. It seems to me that both reasons for removal would be correct."

There was something profoundly comical about the way Sigrid spoke to us, smiling, briefly fixing each of us in her gaze. As if she was messing with us, ridiculing the guidelines—I think that our trainers also wondered for a moment whether she was taking her task seriously. But her answer was correct, and Sigrid's reaction when they told her she'd passed—she laughed and kept nodding over and over, as if she still had to convince herself that she'd done well—showed that she had in fact been serious. This was her way of addressing a crowd, and when she told me weeks later, behind the lockers, that she'd previously worked in the hospitality industry, suddenly her final presentation made sense. (By that point I didn't dare ask her why she'd quit her old line of work. I didn't want to give her any ideas—why was she still here when she could be back pouring beers instead?)

In case you're curious: My own presentation didn't go as well as I'd expected. I got a video of a guy whose arm was on fire. The flames seemed to be spreading to his back, but the fragment was brief and the context was vague. I had them play it again, hoping I'd be able to see how it was the arm caught fire, but no. Was I looking at a violent crime, an accident, a joke, or a political statement? If it was a political statement, the video would need to be left up, and wrongly removing it would be a violation of free speech. I had to ask the trainer to play it a third time, this time with the volume turned all the way up. That was the right move, as it turned out. Everyone could hear the man screaming now, high and shrill like a girl—a sound I'd never forget, but I wasn't thinking about that at the time. No, standing there, in front of the entire cohort, I was mainly just bummed that I hadn't understood sooner what we were dealing with here. It took the edge off my frustration when one girl had to leave the room during her assignment— a video of a man fucking a Rottweiler—and didn't come back until ten minutes later, her eyes red. In the end we were all hired, though, even the girl who walked out.

Alice was the only one who respectfully declined. And maybe my memory is playing tricks on me, but I truly believe that was my greatest disappointment that whole week.

All right. And now for some things I'm sure you're eager to hear about, Mr. Stitic—are you ready? First of all: Everything my former colleagues are saying about our poor working conditions is true. Did we only get two breaks, one for a lousy seven minutes, which ticked away waiting in line for one of the two available restrooms? You bet. Did they give us a hard time if we handled fewer than five hundred tickets a day? Absolutely. Did we get a serious warning the moment our accuracy score dipped below 90 percent? Sure, yes. Did people get fired when they couldn't keep their scores up? Yeah, I've heard stories. A timer that started counting down the moment we left our desks, even if we just went to stretch our legs? That was just how things were at Hexa.

But of course the main thing you want to know is:

What about support for our mental health? Well, where that is concerned I can also back up my colleagues' stories —I barely noticed anything of the sort. Once, we were approached by a counselor, a short guy with fat eyebrows who scurried around in the hallways sometimes and who Sigrid and I started referring to as Super Mario after we spotted him at the bus stop in blue overalls. I'd always thought he was a maintenance guy, but it turned out he'd done some sort of coaching course.

"Is there anything you'd like to get off your chest?" he asked us one day. That was right after there'd been a bit of a situation with Robert. I'd been working for Hexa for a few months at that point. I don't know if they told you about it, but Robert had "gotten a little overworked"—I think that's how Super Mario put it. I noticed it the moment he came in that morning. Normally anyone who walks onto the floor immediately goes in search of a free desk, preferably one without too many sticky spots, ideally by a window. But Robert wasn't looking at the desks by the window— he wasn't looking down at all—because he wasn't looking for somewhere to sit, he was looking for Jaymie, one of our "subject matter experts." Subject matter experts, or SMEs, had to audit our work. They determined our accuracy score based on random samples of our decisions. Although they were essentially our superiors, they sat with all of us moderators. See, I've always found that strange. If I were Hexa, I would've put those SMEs somewhere else, on a separate floor, maybe with bulletproof sliding doors, because now you ended up with a well-meaning guy like Robert walking in on an ordinary Wednesday afternoon, going up to a well-meaning guy like Jaymie, and putting a taser to his back. I'm not even sure what it was about. Robert had removed a post containing a death threat, but Jaymie felt that had been unjustified since the death threat was directed at a public figure, and public figures aren't a protected category, unless they are politicians or activists —or maybe it was the other way around, maybe Robert had left the post up and Jaymie thought the person wasn't a public figure but an activist. Either way, Jaymie had disagreed with Robert's decision and not for the first time— I believe Robert's score had been hovering around the 80 percent mark for a while at that point. And now Robert thought it would be a good idea to threaten Jaymie with an electroshock weapon in order to bring his score back up again. Talk about bad decisions.

This may also be valuable information for you: There was no security on our floor. So Robert just stood there, with that taser between Jaymie's shoulder blades. And

Jaymie didn't move a muscle—at most he said something like "Easy now"—and meanwhile everyone was staring at them, so Robert turned red and Jaymie's neck broke out in blotches, as if they'd been caught in some sort of sexual escapade, the curtain of their canopy bed pulled away and there they were. "Fuck this," Robert finally said. "Fuck you, Jaymie, I'm out of here!"

After that we didn't see Robert for about four days, but the next week he was back in the office, same as usual, albeit with his hood pulled up, but no one asked him to put it down. Everyone knew what had happened, even the people who hadn't been there, and yet Robert had had the balls to come back, to admit, I can't live without Hexa, I can't live without Jaymie, I *need* this job, and you know what, I for one thought that was very big of him.

And now of course you want to know if Robert was offered a session with Super Mario at the time, but I'm sorry, I can't say that with any certainty. All I know is, the day after Robert's outburst Super Mario held court in a room one floor above us—he had his own watercooler and there was a box of tissues on the table. Jesus, so that's really what it's like, I remember thinking: a room with a box of tissues on the table. We were sitting there, thirty people in a circle, about half of the moderators who had been there the morning Robert lost it. I only knew Kyo and Souhaim, who, like Robert, had become friends of mine.

I didn't say anything during that entire session. Because I understood Robert. Our accuracy scores were important—that's what we were in it for. If my own ratings had been consistently low, I would have gotten frustrated too. So I said, "I don't really have anything to say," and I was on the verge of walking out, but then Mario said to me, "I can imagine you may have seen something upsetting at some point."

I'm not joking. He really said that. *I can imagine you may have seen something upsetting at some point.* I looked over at Kyo, who was nodding absentmindedly, and at Souhaim, with whom I exchanged a glance—he subtly raised an eyebrow. It was just insulting, Mario's comment—this guy was trying to win my trust, but he clearly hadn't bothered to do his homework, so no, there was no way I was going to give him anything. Before the end of the session, I got up and went back to my desk, where I spent the rest of the afternoon feeling annoyed because the interruption meant I wouldn't make my targets that day. My colleagues and I never saw Super Mario again—the whole thing was pretty irresponsible, if you ask me.

I do hope you've made notes on all of the above.

. . .

"But how on earth were you able to stand it there under those conditions?" That's what my Aunt Meredith asked when the first newspaper articles about our work came out. I can imagine you're wondering the same thing. All right, then: Before I go on, two reasons.

One: I'd been around the block by the time I started at Hexa. Like I mentioned, I previously worked in a call center, where I was a "customer service assistant" for a third-party company that had been contracted by a large furniture manufacturer that imported their stuff from China or God knows where, so their pink velvet sofas and retro brass side tables would get lost in international distribution centers at least four times before they reached the customer. In the meantime, those customers called me, all day long; my breaks may have been a little longer than at Hexa, but I got paid a lot less, and at the call center too there was a timer that would start counting the moment I got up from my desk, and there too I had to make certain targets, ideally fifteen phone calls an hour but with an average customer satisfaction score of eight and a half—you try to make that number when someone keeps going on about the shipping promises made on the website being legally binding, and how she'd wanted to give that milk-glass table lamp to her daughter for her birthday, and now the whole party was ruined because her present wasn't there. If the success of a birthday party hinges on a milk-glass table lamp, something isn't quite right, you think to yourself, but you don't say that, no, all day long you bite your tongue because if you accidentally say some-thing sensible in reply—"Ma'am, is that really the end of the world?"—they start screaming, yes, at least four in fif-teen customers will start screaming at you and calling you all sorts of names, they'll call you a cunt and then ask for your supervisor . . . your *supervisor*, you don't even know if there *is* a supervisor, you only know Gerry from down-stairs and the woman from the job interview, but of course this is the last thing she'll want to deal with, and as you explain to the customer why you can't connect her to a supervisor right now you just pray that she's in a hurry, that her anger is fueled by stress about all the groceries or children she still has to pick up, and that she'll hang up before the prerecorded female voice can inquire about her customer satisfaction, but no such luck—of course it's always the ones who bitch and moan that rate their expe-rience, and as you're starting to visualize your customer satisfaction score going into free fall, the colleague across from you starts crying because she's having God knows what kind of verbal abuse thrown at her, that poor girl is contorting her face into all kinds of twisted shapes to keep in the noise, and meanwhile you're staring straight into an open mouth strung with saliva.

Long story short: My first few days at Hexa were a breath of fresh air. How wonderful, I thought, how terrific that no one's shouting at me. And yes, the posts I had to review contained the most heinous slurs sometimes—but at least those slurs weren't directed at *me*.

"But how on earth were you able to stand it there under those conditions?"

All right then, here's reason number two: During my first few days on the job, I was a little out of it. My mind was on other things, and work was a welcome distraction, though I didn't talk to my colleagues much at that point, and by the time I'd begun to realize how shitty our working conditions were, I'd already more or less grown used to those conditions—that sounds weird, doesn't it? Let me explain. If you want to understand why I stayed for so long, you need to know how and why it was that I started in the first place.

/ / /

My first real working day at Hexa was a Tuesday. I was
originally supposed to start on Monday, but the only time
Yena could meet me for a drink that week was Monday afternoon at three p.m., so I traded that first shift before I'd
even really begun—I thought it was a miracle they didn't
fire me there and then. Yena was my ex-girlfriend. We'd
met at the call center (I told you I'd been much too friendly
there, didn't I?) and had been together for exactly one year,

seven months of which we'd spent living together in the house I inherited from my mother.

"You've probably been with lots of girls, haven't you?" Yena said the first time she spent the night at my place. We were lying in what had once been my teenage bedroom. It had been years since I'd taken down the Green Day posters and photos of skateboarders, rolled them up, and planted a kiss on them before they disappeared into the storage drawer of the brand-new double bed, and there, in that slightly-too-pimpish four-poster bed, I was now making the fatal mistake of just grinning stupidly at Yena's comment about lots of girls. "So that's a yes, then," she said, and because we both laughed I thought everything was fine. I hadn't been with many girls at all. But I thought: I'll let her believe that, it'll probably make me more attractive to her.

The truth was that I'd only been in one long-term relationship before Yena. Barbra was fifteen years older; we'd met when I was seventeen and my mother had just been hospitalized for the second time—I'll leave the psychological interpretation up to you, Mr. Stitic. By the time my mother died I was already living with Barbra. I rented out my childhood home (which was now mine, as my father had backed out of the driveway for the final time a few years earlier) to a bunch of students until, six years later, Barbra asked me how I would feel if her new lover, a massage therapist named Lilian who was barely twenty years old, were to move in with us. All I can say is we parted very amicably. We cleaved apart cleanly like two halves of a cake, the knife separating us with careful precision so that none of the marzipan roses were damaged. Barbra helped me find a polite way to evict the tenants from my mother's house, and as I was packing the wheeled suitcases that she'd bought for me especially—she didn't want me to go lugging boxes or trash bags—I realized that, more than anything, I felt relief: Deep down I'd always known that I would never have the balls to leave the woman who had done so much for me.

I felt free during those first few days by myself in the house where I'd learned to talk and play the guitar. I did the things I'd never been allowed to do when I still lived there, letting the trash bags pile up on the porch and having pizza rolls for breakfast, lunch, and dinner—as if I was trying to tell the house that it was mine now, I was the lord and master, from now on I'd be making the rules. I spent days on end gaming, lying in bed by myself or on the couch with Mehran, who was still my best friend back then. But then the fridge stopped working. The lawnmower had been sitting broken in the shed for a while—the grass had grown up to the porch. The washing machine was leaking so badly that the bathroom flooded every time I ran a load; I'd started wearing panty liners to save underwear. "You need new stuff," Mehran said one afternoon when I offered him a tub of watery cream cheese. "It's not healthy, having a broken fridge," and he looked at me sternly until I finally admitted I couldn't afford a new one.

So that's how I'd ended up at the call center. Before Yena asked me out, I'd made out with Lorna a couple of times (who I suspect was mainly hoping that getting cozy with me on the dance floor would turn Mitch on), and I think that's why Yena was trying to suss out if I'd already been with a lot of girls. And my God, how I ended up regretting not telling her the truth right away. *One woman, I've only been with one other woman, and during the last three years of our relationship our sex life was nonexistent*—but no, I didn't say that. I let Yena believe I was some kind of Casanova, and from that moment on, pretty much every time we saw a woman on TV or on our phones she'd ask me what I thought of her. How attractive did I find this girl, on a one-to-ten scale, what about her lips, if I had to rate those separately, and was that woman's ass a lot rounder than hers? And the gorgeous lead actress from that cop show, what if she suddenly appeared in front of you, would you try to hit on her? And what about that weather girl, and the woman living next door, and her own sister, did I find her attractive, and who did I find the most attractive, her or her sister? No, that was going too far, wasn't it? "Haha, just kidding," Yena would say.

I began to realize it wasn't me that was the problem. It was the beauty standards society imposed on us, self-loathing and abandonment issues going back to child-hood, yada yada, the stuff of women's magazines, but I still felt responsible somehow. Yena's insecurities were soap bubbles that I had to keep popping, like in that game you play on your phone, but new ones kept appearing and I didn't want to lose, I didn't want to lose *her*, because she laughed at my jokes and told me I was beautiful and she understood what was so good about not all but *some* cop shows, and at night, when she was lying with her head against my chest, which fit exactly because she was so petite, she made my heart beat slower—yes, slower, and that was exactly what I needed. So when, after our first couple of weeks together, she started asking me for things—very subtly, almost casually—I saw her wishes as welcome pointers: useful, concrete instructions for ways to prove my love.

A big TV so that we didn't have to watch our shows on my buggy laptop anymore—hey, wouldn't we both benefit from that? A sofa bed, so that her sister didn't have to drive the ninety miles back to her place every time. That dress with the puffy sleeves, because she'd lost weight and all her other clothes reminded her of her old self. Those high-waisted pants, because she'd gained weight and didn't feel pretty in anything else. Maybe we should have a proper meal out sometime, in that restaurant with all the climbing plants that we kept seeing in other people's pictures, because we hadn't seen much of each other recently, and wasn't next week our seven-month anniversary? A trip to Paris, maybe, because we were arguing so much, and hadn't I been the one to say we just needed to get away for a bit? That turntable so she could practice at home—this was sure to be a very lucrative side hustle, and it was high time she started putting herself first. A wig, two wigs, because of course she needed an image, and a decent camera while we were at it, because of course she had to promote that image with some professional-level PR. By the way, if she had a car she'd be able to get to gigs much faster, and if she had a better phone we could at least video chat if she had to go on a long trip at some point, and shit, that club where she was supposed to play hadn't sold enough tickets and apparently if the show had to be canceled she had to cover part of the costs herself, those assholes with their fine print—did I happen to have it in cash, by any chance?

"She's using you," Mehran said one night when Yena wasn't there. We were playing a new first-person shooter he'd brought and Mehran had just shot a bunch of zombies in the head.

"She's not using me, I'm helping her with her new career," I muttered as I reloaded my weapon.

"She's only got, like, forty followers on social," Mehran said, taking cover behind a barrel of gasoline.

"That kind of thing takes time."

"She's a gold digger."

"Gold digger?" I laughed and shot down a helicopter, shaking my head: "Dude, I don't even *have* anything!"

"See, that's the problem," Mehran said, "and you know it," and he lowered his controller to try to meet my eyes, allowing me to win the game.

Okay, Mr. Stitic, now you have some idea of the events that led me to apply for a job with Hexa. I was pretty much bankrupt when I walked into that coffee shop the Monday before I was supposed to start. I hadn't seen Yena in two months and I honestly thought I was over her—to Mehran's relief, I'd even begun to feel some resentment. But when I saw her sitting there, dwarfed by the low table, hunched over her phone, I felt my stomach go into free fall. She'd done something with her eyebrows, I'd already seen it in her profile picture—they were a lot fuller all of a sudden, the individual hairs merged into thick black bars above her eyes, as if her forehead had been redacted. I didn't like it, but I remember thinking it was sweet how much effort she'd put into it. Meanwhile, she was telling me how sorry she was. She was sorry and she missed me.

I missed her too, I said. And I told her about my new job, and that my debts weren't an issue anymore because I'd made an arrangement with the credit card company, but she didn't respond to that. Yena pretended my debts didn't exist, like a guy who gets his girlfriend pregnant and then blames her for not taking the pill: My debts were my problem, the bastard child she wanted nothing to do with. Of course, that was dickish behavior, but by the time we said goodbye with a hug and a kiss on the mouth that lasted a beat too long, I was way past blaming her for anything— the magic words "I miss you" had done their work. Maybe we should try again after all. But this time we shouldn't move in together right away; we should take it slow, split the bills. Believe it or not, those were the kinds of things that I spent my first few days at Hexa thinking about.

During each break I hurried over to the lockers to check my phone, to see if Yena had texted me back yet. I stood there like a shivering junkie with the few other colleagues who were crazy enough to trade one screen for another. Cell phones were strictly forbidden on the floor, because they didn't want us to take any pictures or video of the content we reviewed, and over there, in the huddle by the lockers, I felt like nothing less than a soldier at a battlefield post office, hoping for a new passport photo of his sweetheart, a little note letting him know she was thinking about him. The weird thing was, when this soldier was on leave from the front for a day, it proved rather difficult to meet with that girl. She had to play a set in a club I couldn't find any information about. Or she'd be staying over at her sister's again and wouldn't be back until the next day. She wasn't getting my messages because her phone was broken—what a bad buy that had turned out to be, she really should get a new one, wink, wink.

"Enough with her already," Mehran said one Friday evening. He put a hand between my shoulder blades, more of a steadying gesture than a comforting one—a father's hand on the back of a son learning to ride a bike. "You deserve better," he said, and this time I didn't protest.

When I went back to work that Sunday, I picked a locker close to the ground so I wouldn't be able to get at my phone so easily, and that day I went outside during the break for the first time in weeks, into the crisp cold. It was late November—my colleagues stood in small groups around the parking lot, leaning against walls or lampposts, the sun was low and cast their long shadows across the asphalt. People were busy with what I still believed to be cigarettes and bottled water—for a moment I was twelve years old again with no idea which schoolyard clique I was supposed to join, until I spotted Sigrid, Kyo, and a guy in a hoodie who I didn't know sitting on a wall, a kind of ledge that separated the parking lot from the driveway.

"Hey," I called out as I headed over there. "Hey," Sigrid said immediately. "You're Kayleigh, right?" She smiled and tugged at her gloves. They were too small and the sleeves of her coat too short, so her wrists remained bare no matter how hard she pulled—it would be some time before I realized this fidgeting with her gloves was a nervous tic. In that moment, Sigrid mainly just looked very cool in her tight leather jacket. "So we've got a dilemma," she said, motioning for me to sit down on the wall next to her. "Robert over here just saw a video of some nutjob playing with two dead kittens on his bed. So there's no graphic animal cruelty taking place, because they're already dead when the video begins." Sigrid glanced over at Robert, the guy in the hoodie. I wondered why he wasn't wearing a coat in this weather, and Robert nodded, his shoulders hunched against the cold. "They were completely stiff," he mumbled, and Sigrid went on: "You might think: Leave it up, it's not fundamentally different from those pictures of dead guinea pigs posted by their grieving owners. But!"

"That nutjob previously posted a video in which you can actually see him killing those kittens," Kyo chimed in. He was parroting her use of the word "nutjob" and his voice cracked on the word "killing" like he was going through puberty—not much older than seventeen, I thought for the second time.

"Which means that graphic animal cruelty, subcategory violent death, *has taken* place," Sigrid said. "That guy suffocated those kittens and maybe even broke their necks, but you wouldn't know that unless you happened to have seen the previous video, so what do you do with a video that only shows him *playing* with those dead creatures?"

"Leave it up," I immediately said. Sigrid, Kyo, and Robert gave me a searching look—for a moment, I felt like an oracle. "Provided there's no cruel caption, that is. If there's no text, it complies with the guidelines—that previous video doesn't count. Jaymie can't give you any shit for leaving it up."

Sigrid nodded. "Told you so," she said, and Kyo smiled, relieved, perhaps, that the discussion was over, but Robert just shook his head. "Goddammit, so I screwed up after all," he said, and lit a roll-up cigarette with slightly trembling fingers.

Robert, Kyo, Sigrid. And later on, Souhaim and Louis, too. Those were the people who would come to mean the most to me during my months at Hexa—I would grow to genuinely love them. Sigrid and the guys had been friendly for a while, though I never entirely understood what bound them together. Maybe it was the same thing that had drawn me to them: our working conditions, in the broadest sense of the term. Like me, Kyo, Souhaim, and Sigrid belonged to the October cohort, which was doing reasonably well at this point. I shared most of my shifts with Robert, Louis, and, again, Sigrid, which meant that Sigrid and I saw a bit more of Louis, for example, than we did of Souhaim, who sometimes also worked night shifts. My new colleagues were the only people who knew what I saw during the day, what that felt like, and what that meant, although we didn't talk much about that last part; during working hours, we mainly talked about what to take down and what to leave up. Sometimes one of us would say, "I just saw something really fucked up, dude," and the rest of us would nod and know to leave them alone for a bit. Outside working hours, however, it was a completely different story. Do you want to know what things were like then? Well, all right—allow me to take you along to our local bar.

A sports bar, one bus stop away from our business park, next to a home improvement store, a car dealership, and two fast food joints that are embroiled in bitter competition, which is why they've both recently started offering free soda with their all-you-can-eat deals. It's December, Christmas Eve, as a matter of fact—I've been working at

Hexa for two months now and ever since that first cigarette break on the wall with Sigrid, Robert, and Kyo, I've
spent every evening here, knocking back B-52s. After a
harsh November, the weeks leading up to the holidays
have been mild but rainy. We even have a Christmas tree
in the lobby at Hexa, and string lights are blinking in the
windows of the sports bar—at this point I don't know yet
that those lights are always there. Louis does know, because he's been working at Hexa for more than a year. He
often complains about the turnover rate: We have to promise we'll stay, he tells us from time to time, and of course
we're flattered by that. Next to him is Souhaim, who is a
little older than the rest of us and has a degree in French.
Before this, Souhaim did freelance translation work, but
business dried up and eventually he spent most of his
time on HITs, human intelligence tasks: small online jobs
farmed out by companies who paid him a paltry sum for
each medication package insert or oven instruction man-
ual he translated. At Hexa they promised him a swift pro-
motion, maybe to SME for the French market, but whenever Souhaim asks about it no one is able to tell him when
that will happen—but I don't know any of that yet either,
on this Christmas Eve, because Souhaim rarely talks about
himself. He prefers to expound on the differences in qual-

ity between various kinds of beer. He's also very generous when it comes to buying rounds. We can barely keep up with him and tonight, too, we pour our leftovers into each other's half-empty glasses: Whoever has the least gets the most, that happens automatically, the routine part of our rapport.

Listen, "All I Want for Christmas" is playing on the radio. On the highway behind us, people are stuck in traffic on the way to their families, the churches are filling up for Mass, for prayers over plastic mangers and perhaps reflections on the past year, and what is the subject of our conversations this evening, what are we talking about, sitting there on our bar stools?

About nothing at all. Yes, we're talking and we're laughing and we're finally relaxing, thank God, pointing at the game, a rerun, on the screen above us. As always, Louis is shouting the loudest, and even before he's lifted his second beer to his mouth he's yelling that it's high time that slow-ass pussy learned to run.

"God, he's such a lazy fucking faggot, they're never gonna score like this, they're taking even longer to crush their opponents than it took Hitler to crush the Jews—you guys, *look* at what just walked in here. No, don't look right away, you idiots, yes, *now,* at three o'clock, there she is, just look at that, do you think anyone's ever tapped that without throwing up in his mouth after? As long as she doesn't come and sit over here with her three hundred pounds . . . We won't be able to see a thing—hey, Robert, go and take that empty stool before that dyke beats us to it!"

And just look at us laughing. Yeah, we all laugh, even though Kyo is a little overweight ("baby fat" is what we call it), I'm a dyke, Souhaim is black, and Louis himself is Jewish—time and again we laugh at these kinds of jokes, out of habit but also out of recognition, because this is the kind of language that gay people, Jews, people of color, immigrants, and whatever other PCs you can think of get thrown at them, the kind of language, in other words, that we spend all day at work dealing with. Are we ridiculing that language when we say that the bar must have been taken over by Jews, because look how tiny the portions of chicken nuggets are these days?

I wish I could say yes, but it's not that simple. Okay, the fact that we employ this kind of humor *is* a joke in and of itself—that is, we know full well that it's pretty

ironic to be saying the very things we spent all day ex-
cising from the platform—but our cracks aren't some sort
of moral commentary so much as an exciting flirtation
with the forbidden. And maybe they're also just a way to
prove how tough we are, how resilient, to ourselves and
to each other: God no, we're not letting our job damage us
or anything, no way—though if you heard us talking like
this, you might think the opposite, and maybe I'm reading too much into it now, that's not impossible, maybe the
others had always found jokes about slow-ass faggots hi-
larious. Either way, I don't think any of us feel offended.
Souhaim is the only one who will occasionally say something like "Not cool, dude," with that raised eyebrow of
his that could indicate either irritation or indifference. On
this Christmas Eve, it's our favorite bartender who gen-
tly intervenes. "On the house," Michelle says, putting a
tray full of shots down on the table. "Remember, peace on
Earth and all that, okay?"

"Yeah, man, peace on fucking Earth," we say as we curl
our hands into unnatural positions to clink the minuscule
glasses, the fluorescent drinks sloshing over the rims and
leaving us with sticky hands for the rest of the evening.

· · ·

It was Kyo, the baby of the group, who used the word "friend" for the first time. It happened after an incident in late January. It had been dark for days on end, and we were pretty depressed and worn out—a lot of moderators had been off for the holidays, and the rest of us had worked double or even triple shifts. "Look!" someone—Louis, I think—shouted suddenly. "There's someone up there!"

We looked outside, and he was right: There was a man standing on the roof of the building opposite, not even that far away—I think he would have fit exactly between my outstretched thumb and forefinger. The man took a step forward, toward the edge, and we got up, all eighty of us, even Jaymie and the two other SMEs. We stood there, crowded around the window, as the timers on our screens ticked away. The man took a step back now—was he about to take a running start? From where we were standing, we had a clear view of where he'd end up: There were only a few cars in the parking lot. That convertible might break his fall, I thought in a flash. In videos of this sort of thing you usually didn't see the ground, in which case we could leave them up, but this wasn't a stunt or a joke or some activist making a statement. We would definitely see blood and maybe even bits of his insides, so this isn't allowed, I remember thinking, and maybe some of the others were thinking the same thing but no one said anything, until Louis shouted, "Jesus Christ, motherfucker, jump already!" Some people laughed nervously, but Louis's face froze. His voice had cracked with anxiety on the word "motherfucker," and he knew we'd all heard it. "We have to do something," someone said, and although people immediately started murmuring in agreement, no one did anything.

But then what could we do? We didn't have our phones on us, our department didn't even have landlines—the platform was clearly terrified that we'd go and rat out misbehaving users (who on earth would we rat them out to?). I looked over at Jaymie, but he didn't seem about to go get his phone from his locker either. We all stood there completely frozen, staring at the roof as if we would be able to catch and save the man with just our gaze.

I looked down again, and only then did I see her. Four stories below us, someone was walking across our own parking lot toward the other side. "Who is that?" I said quietly, but I already knew who it was, though I could hardly believe it. That whole time it was like I'd been watching a video, and now all of a sudden someone I knew had appeared on screen, someone who'd been standing next to me just moments earlier—like in that horror movie about the girl who comes out of the TV, except in reverse.

"Hey, that's Sigrid!" Kyo said, and he sounded excited, as if the horse he'd bet on was suddenly taking the lead. We were all looking at her now, a little black ball that rolled toward the building on the other end of the parking lot, until it was swallowed up by two large glass sliding doors. I could feel my neck growing hot. Was Sigrid going to get there on time? And why hadn't it occurred to me to go down there?

We looked back at the roof. "Wow," the people around me gasped, because a second man had appeared. Now the two men crouched down simultaneously. They seemed to be kneeling before something, a higher being that would bestow its blessing on them from up in the gray January sky, but they weren't looking up, they were looking down, and now they started pounding away at something with a violent, almost theatrical flailing of their arms.

"Fuck me," Louis said, "they're just construction workers!" There was still a tremor in his voice.

"Jesus," other people chimed in, "fucking construction workers," and it sounded angry, as if the man on the roof had been crying out for help, as if he'd deliberately deceived us. We went back to our desks as quickly as we'd gotten up, where we discovered we'd let nine valuable minutes tick away.

By the time Sigrid reappeared, we were all back at work. She must have suspected that we already knew the score, and yet she stopped in the doorway. "Okay, guys," she said, loudly and with clear enunciation, "everything's fine. They're just fixing the roof."

A few of us nodded—"Okay, good to know, thanks, Sigrid"—but Louis, of course Louis started shouting again. "Thanks for nothing, bitch, we already knew that!"

He didn't mean it in a bad way—for us, "bitch" was more of a term of endearment—but Kyo still got to his feet. He marched resolutely over to Louis's desk. Everyone looked up. "Get a grip, man," Kyo said. "That's no way to talk to a friend"—and before Louis could reply, Kyo kept on going, toward Sigrid, who was still standing in the doorway. He put his arms around her and she accepted his solemn embrace and for the second time in fifteen minutes, I cursed myself for not having taken action—all these opportunities to be the hero and all I'd done was sit here and watch.

During the break, the mood was different than usual, albeit in a nice way: We were giddy, yelling, maybe even giggling. That man on the roof had scared the shit out of us, but it turned out everything was fine, and what we were feeling now was a mixture of relief and sweet self-pity, because what had led us to believe that man was going to jump?

"The gazillion videos of jumpers that we've seen," Robert muttered as he sat down on our wall, his eyes red, and we nodded, probably feeling equal parts noble and sorry for ourselves. Robert passed around his rollie. By now I knew there was an inordinate amount of hash in his tobacco and normally I turned them down, but this time even I took a drag, this time we all took a drag, Robert, Sigrid, Souhaim, Kyo, and even Louis, and I'm sure that as we did Kyo's words from that afternoon rang through our heads: *That's no way to talk to a friend*—a friend, yes, we were *friends*, I don't think that had been stated so clearly before, and it felt like something had been formal-ized, owned up to: In the heat of the battle, love had been smoked out of its hideout, or something like that.

I looked over at Sigrid. She was about to take a third drag. I looked at her tight ponytail, her long, thin fingers which were already passing the spliff on to Louis and then unscrewing the lid off a tin of lip balm. Who was this woman? What did I even know about her?

I looked for a second too long. Sigrid caught me and smiled reproachfully.

That night we ended up kissing for the first time. After work Robert passed around another rollie, and at the bus stop we all took a swig from Souhaim's stylish horn hip flask, so when we walked into the sports bar around seven we were still in high spirits—in fact, we were whooping as if we'd all won in the Olympics. Inside, some people were dancing. That was a rare sight in the sports bar, but Michelle must have picked up on her clientele's mood and had cranked up the volume on the playlist all the way. One girl from our cohort was making out with a huge guy. It took me a moment to recognize him—it was John, who always wore blue gingham button-downs in the office, but who was now swaying his hips in a soaking wet T-shirt, the fabric drenched with sweat even though it wasn't very warm inside or outside.

I don't dance, so I sat down on one of the last free bar stools. Sigrid came up next to me. The music was too loud to be able to talk and, by implication, too loud to turn down shots, and to be honest, my memory of our first kiss is pretty blurry. Later, during the spell when Sigrid and I didn't see each other for a while, I would nonetheless evoke that kiss when I was masturbating, and over time my memory of the fantasy has become clearer than my memory of the night itself. In that fantasy Sigrid won't stop staring at me. She uses every excuse to touch me, deliberately pressing into me as she leans over to grab another beer off the tray. In the fantasy, I reach out and put a hand on her thigh; she, in turn, shakes her head and flushes red, and then I get up to go to the restroom and she follows me. She tugs at my shoulder to turn me toward her and I push her up against the wall. We're blocking the hallway to the restrooms, which is too narrow as it is—by the time our lips touch I've usually already come, and if not, I switch to a different memory, an image from a few weeks later: We're in my bed and Sigrid is straddling me, "Deeper, deeper," she cries, her face contorted with pleasure and yet vaguely mournful, and the memory of that grimace—ugly and hot at the same time—tends to get me there right away. But if you asked me what our first kiss actually looked like, I suspect it wasn't much different from John in his wet T-shirt making out with that girl from my cohort. Two people who know somewhere deep down that they're probably being watched but who feed off each other's energy, and so they end up rolling all the way down the side of that mountain, the alcohol their gravity. "You guys just kept going at it," Kyo said the next morning. "You just kept making out all night long!" He sounded positively elated, as if we were his divorced parents who'd just rekindled their love: I think we all laughed, not least at the contrast between Kyo's enthusiasm and our bleary, hungover faces.

When did my interest in Sigrid turn romantic? I find it difficult to pinpoint the exact moment—we were both kind of blasé about that first kiss. But it still made me hungry for more. That week, whenever someone suggested going to the sports bar, before she agreed Sigrid would check if I was up for it too, which made me go all weak in the knees. We kissed more and more often—on the nights when we didn't end up making out, I'd lie in bed afterward wondering if maybe I hadn't been forward enough, only to be covered in shame the next morning because I suddenly felt sure I'd actually been trying too hard. I started drinking more—sometimes even on the breaks, but definitely by the time we got to the bus stop. But then we all started drinking more. One afternoon Sigrid downed all of Souhaim's hip flask in a single gulp, after which Louis applauded and Souhaim feigned a dirty look.

One morning, one or two weeks after that first kiss, Sigrid suddenly told me she wouldn't be coming along to the sports bar that evening. I was startled, I felt caught out and mocked: Why was she telling me this at nine a.m., and why did she sound so apologetic? Had I been that obvious? To prove that I didn't care whether or not she was there, after work I went to the sports bar with just Robert and Louis. We didn't have much to talk about, but the good thing was that I hardly had anything to drink that night and went home early so I could get myself off before going to sleep, which meant that the next morning I arrived at work without a hangover for the first time in days.

"Hey, I'm coming with you guys again tonight," Sigrid whispered in my ear when we were walking to our usual hangout in the parking lot that afternoon. Though I was happy about that prospect, I felt slightly insulted. "Whatever you want," I said as flatly as possible, and then Sigrid did something she'd never done before. There, on our wall, she grabbed my hand for the first time. It almost seemed like a throwaway gesture, as casually as you might pull your phone out of your pocket. She didn't even look at me, she kept on talking to Souhaim about who knows what. For a moment, I wanted to jerk away, but instead I started squeezing. It happened almost automatically: I gripped her fingers with all my might, until she couldn't have let go even if she'd wanted to.

Was that the moment? The moment I truly fell in love? Maybe not, Mr. Stitic. Maybe falling in love isn't filling up a loyalty card with feelings and actions so much as just adding two things together: desire plus fear. The desire had appeared fairly suddenly—ever since that first kiss, really. The fear, on the other hand, grew gradually: fear that she wouldn't be coming to the sports bar that night, fear that we wouldn't end up kissing, fear that she'd change her mind. Those were pretty much the stages of falling in love for me.

The first time we had sex wasn't memorable. The first time we woke up together was, even though it was a quarter past six in the fucking morning because I'd taken on a super early shift. It was still dark out when I walked into the nearest gas station to get coffee and chocolate muffins. The two other customers saw a gray figure with hunched shoulders coming through the door; I may have even looked suspect to them in my sweatpants and black hoodie. But man, there was a gorgeous woman in my bed, and when it was my turn to pay I was so euphoric that I told the boy at the cash register to keep the change, even though it was almost enough for a pack of cigarettes.

/ / /

"Tell me a little bit about your relationship," Dr. Ana said during our second session.

We were sitting in an office that looked suspiciously like a living room, and I wondered whether Dr. Ana sat here by herself in the evenings reading the paper. There was art on the wall and no box of tissues on the table, and Dr. Ana had told me I could take off my shoes if I liked but I'd kept them on.

"What do you want me to tell you?" I asked.

"Whatever comes to mind," Dr. Ana said, warming her hands on her tea glass.

"I don't know what it is you want to hear," I said, and Dr. Ana kept smiling encouragingly and said there were no right or wrong answers.

I must have seemed like some kind of redneck who didn't want to participate in her own therapy. That wasn't necessarily true—Aunt Meredith had set this up and I felt like I owed it to her (and her wallet) to give Dr. Ana a chance. Besides, I knew that it's usually easier to get things like this over with if you go along with them, and you know what, I *liked* Dr. Ana, I liked how she'd made me tea. But I had to be careful. By then it had been two months since I'd left Hexa, and I hadn't seen Sigrid since. What did the woman sitting across from me want me to share? What did she think she'd be able to dig up?

"What kinds of things did the two of you do together?" Dr. Ana asked. I stared at the painting behind her, a dark figure, more shadow than human being, reaching for something with arms like wooden sticks. Maybe it was that strange artwork, maybe it was Dr. Ana's empathic silence, but suddenly it felt like something black and sticky was seeping into my body.

"We did the same things together that we used to do by

ourselves," I finally said. "Working, sleeping, and going to the sports bar"—and that was true, Mr. Stitic.

It just wasn't the whole story.

Sigrid was five years older than me. She lived in a small but tastefully furnished apartment that we never went to. She didn't want children, she didn't have any debts, she'd had a seven-year relationship with a man who she was still on good terms with, not least because they shared custody of a German shepherd; the dog lived with her ex, Pete, because his house was bigger. Every other Sunday, Sigrid went for a walk around the lake with Pete the ex and Mickey the dog (and oh, how I melted when I saw pictures of her with that huge wolf). Sigrid had no regrets, she often said. Okay, there was one: She'd never gotten a degree. At seventeen, she didn't want to stay in school any longer and her parents had readily agreed with her when she told them she wasn't cut out for college. She still resented them for that; their advice had probably been motivated by financial concerns, she said, but she said it so often that I began to suspect she maybe wasn't entirely convinced it was true. She'd spent years working in bars,

she'd been demoted from dancer to bartender, she joked—
but her knee had started to give out, she was sick of working late shifts, and she was hoping she'd be able to use her
job at Hexa to fund a college education further down the
line.

That was part of the reason why we stopped going
to the sports bar as much. It was cheaper to get drunk
at home. Besides, after our first night together, secretly I
didn't want to have to share Sigrid with the guys all the
time—I wanted to really get to know her, find out everything about her, stop wasting our scant free time having conversations about disallowed goals and the size of
European pint glasses versus American ones. And okay,
maybe I also liked being in bed before nine sometimes so I
wouldn't be too tired to get her off properly.

Sigrid was very different from Yena. "I'm cooking tonight," she announced after just a few days. For a moment I thought I'd landed some sort of domestic goddess,
but that conclusion proved premature—that night, the
pasta was mushy and the tomato sauce much too watery.
When I'd finished my plate, to my astonishment Sigrid
burst out laughing. "Sorry, but this was a total disaster. I
never thought you would actually eat it!" I laughed too,
surprised and relieved, but also somewhat ashamed. I'd

pretended to like the meal because I thought Sigrid might get mad at me if I didn't (Yena definitely would've gotten mad). Thankfully, she interpreted my reaction differently: "It's so sweet that you didn't want to hurt my feelings," she kept saying for the rest of the evening.

Sigrid seemed very confident—she was different from Yena in that regard, too. She clearly knew what she was doing and what she wanted, no "Let's take it one step at a time" or "Why don't we wait and see"—she'd picked *me*, the cutest puppy from the litter, and she didn't seem to have a shred of doubt as to how exactly I felt about *her*. Not that she needed to, because that sense of certainty was exactly what I found so alluring—it only made her rise in my esteem, although I remained a little on guard during that honeymoon period, especially when Sigrid started buying groceries for us two or three times a week. She knew I had debts and insisted on paying for everything—she wouldn't have accepted so much as a tomato from me. And yet the first few times she put her white plastic shopping bags down on my kitchen counter I found it hard to believe she wasn't going to pull out a receipt after all at some point, and for weeks I set aside money just in case. But Sigrid never asked me for anything—the opposite, in fact: After we'd been together for six weeks, she asked me what I wanted for my upcoming birthday, my twenty-seventh. "Nothing!" I said, because I knew what kind of money she was making and I knew what she was saving up for. I had her swear she wouldn't buy me anything and she kept that promise, although she ended up presenting me with an amazing gift, which melted away the last vestiges of my apprehension.

We both had that morning off and she'd made breakfast: toast, eggs, orange juice, the whole deal. There was an envelope leaning against my mug: "An email from my vet," Sigrid said.

"What? Why?"

"Go on, read it!"

It was so freaking sweet. God, I could have cried when I read that email, because it was about something that had happened when I was a kid, something I'd only told Sigrid.

The story of my hamster, Archibalt.

I was seven years old when I got the little guy. Archibalt was actually fairly big for a hamster. He had huge eyes and a thick, soft coat of golden fur, so cute and pretty that if you saw him in pictures, you'd wonder if he was real. Whenever I got home from school, he would pull himself up on the bars of his cage with his front paws and

swing his little body toward his barred ceiling in a maneu-
ver that was nothing short of acrobatic. He'd hang there
upside down like a sloth—his customary way of greeting me. I'd reward him with a piece of toast, which he
would stuff into his cheeks as soon as his little feet were
safely back on the sawdust. Every night I sat by his cage
and I'd tell him which kids from my class had and hadn't
wanted to talk to me that day—and a year or two later,
I'd also update him on how my mother was doing and
what my father had said the doctor had said. Archibalt always listened. He'd close his eyes when I scratched him
behind the ears with my forefinger. And when I think
about how much effort it must have taken him to do those
calisthenics for me day after day, I still feel the need to
hug him close: "Oh, Archibalt!" I sighed the first time I
told Sigrid about him. She'd just shown me a picture of
Mickey the German shepherd, and I think we were in
the stage of a relationship when it still kind of feels like
you're interviewing each other at times—we'd have the
kinds of long conversations that reveal that the amount
of love you feel for each other isn't exactly commensu-
rate with the amount of information you have about each
other: I think we were trying to bridge the gap by asking questions, and I told Sigrid everything I could re-

member about Archibalt, even how our time together had ended.

One afternoon my father had picked me up from school earlier than usual. My mother was having surgery —he warned me that it was going to be a long night. At eleven thirty we were still sitting in the waiting room. My father asked if I wanted him to take me home, and I thought of Archibalt, who'd been scurrying around in his sawdust by himself for hours by then. But my father seemed tired and the look in his eyes told me that he'd really rather not make the trip; he'd be sleeping in the hospital and I think I didn't want to spend the night alone either, to be honest. By the time we got back the following afternoon, Archibalt hadn't had anything to eat in almost forty-eight hours. When I walked into my room and he commenced his usual aerial routine, I was pleasantly surprised. There he was, my fierce little Archibalt, proudly upside down. But when I held a piece of toast in front of his face he barely reacted. I gingerly stroked his head, and the way I remember it he responded by closing his little eyes, slowly but with dignity. Then his little body suddenly started trembling, like that of a runner barely making it over the finish line. I hurriedly lifted him out of his cage and put him in my lap. Archibalt was so light it was as if there was a plum lying on my knees, he'd always been like that—but this time the plum didn't roll around the way it usually did. This time my plum lay still, never to open his little eyes again.

I always knew it was my fault, and when I told Sigrid about the sin I'd committed at almost eleven years old, it felt as if I was letting her into the basement of my soul. But Sigrid didn't seem shocked or surprised—pensive, if anything, as if I'd presented her with an algebra problem I couldn't work out. "Hmm," she said. "But hamsters can go a little while without food, can't they? How old did you say Archibalt was?" She said something else about how it probably wasn't my fault, and I thought it was sweet but I didn't believe her, of course, and now, on my birthday, suddenly I found that letter in front of my steaming mug of coffee.

"Provided that the cage wasn't placed in direct sunlight or exposed to a draft," I read, "it is, in fact, possible and even probable that the animal died of old age. As a rule, hamsters can easily go two days without food. They tend to have a stash hidden somewhere"—signed, the vet who'd neutered Sigrid's German shepherd at one point.

It was the best present anyone had ever given me, but I didn't tell her that. I think I was afraid it wouldn't sound believable and that I would only end up offending Sigrid with my awkward stammering. I let her pull me into a hug, and I spent the rest of the day thinking about the letter, which meant that at work I just sat there with a silly smile on my face as I watched a video of a man in red coveralls being shot in the back by an invisible assailant in the distance.

"And how exactly did you feel when you were with her?"

I think that was Dr. Ana's next question, that afternoon when we were talking about Sigrid.

"How did I feel?" I asked.

"Yes, how did you feel when you were with her?"

"I felt good. I felt on top of the world."

"Why do you think that was?"

It was probably because of stupid, corny-ass reasons —things that, if I were to mention them, would not only be an insult to Sigrid but also to my own eloquence, and I didn't want Dr. Ana to think that I was some kind of simpleton just because our conversation was somewhat strained. So I went ahead and told her about Sigrid's birthday present and Dr. Ana wrote something on her notepad, blew on her tea, and nodded as if she'd been there herself, as if I was refreshing *her* memory with my recollections: "That all sounds lovely," she said.

I nodded, took a sip of my own tea, and suddenly swelled with pride. A strange kind of pride, as if I'd taken a difficult exam and Dr. Ana had just told me I'd aced it. For a moment I was relieved, but when I was walking back to the subway after our appointment, that feeling ebbed away. It had been stupid of me to tell Dr. Ana about Sigrid. I quickened my pace, didn't look back, and turned my phone off. As if I could be getting a call from a disappointed Dr. Ana at any moment, letting me know she was failing me after all because she'd found out I'd copied my answers off someone else.

I think we'd been together for seven weeks when Sigrid read a book about nutrition and the mind. We needed more vegetables, she said, and a lot more protein and fatty acids: "That'll make us feel better before we know it." I didn't ask her that night what she meant by "That'll make us feel better before we know it." Instead I said, only half teasing, "But, baby, we drink at least four cans of beer every night. That's not exactly good for us either."

"But we *need* that," Sigrid said decisively, after which I was smart enough to keep quiet.

Within a few days, a large box was delivered. Sigrid had ordered eleven bags of goji berries and some other dried fruit and seeds. "Acai and chia," she said, "good for our heads."

I watched, frowning, as she shoved tea bags with different flavors into one box to make room for her new supplies in my kitchen cabinet. "How much did those berries cost?" I heard myself say. "You could probably just as well have bought blueberries." But Sigrid firmly shook her head. "These have extra healing properties—they're super healthy."

"More like super well-marketed," I said, but Sigrid shrugged and closed the kitchen cabinet with a touch of solemnity, as if the berries in there had to be left alone so their special powers could grow undisturbed.

That evening Sigrid was a lot quieter than usual. When I asked her if anything was the matter she said she had a stomachache, so I made her a hot water bottle.

As the spring progressed, Sigrid and I found ourselves having more and more goji berry moments. Sigrid had downloaded a meditation app and suggested I do the same: "Maybe it'll help you, too," she said. I laughed and said I didn't believe you could meditate on a phone. "Okay" was all she said in response, and she demonstratively deleted the app in front of me, but a few days later I saw the meditation logo flash by on her screen again and suddenly I understood how that pillow had ended up in the middle of the living room floor earlier that day.

Not long after, she got properly angry with me for the first time. We were standing in the parking lot in front of our office tower, and Robert wasn't doing too well. This was right before all that stuff with the taser, and Robert had stopped passing around his "cigarettes"—we'd been watching for a few days as he smoked his infamous creations by himself. "I don't know how much longer I can stand it here like this," Robert said, and we nodded. We knew what he was talking about—the week before, we'd received some pretty bad news. From now on, porn and spam would be forwarded directly to a new team of moderators in India. We'd be focusing mainly on violence, abuse, and other "culturally sensitive issues"—threats, posts where the boundary between irony and racism was blurry, that kind of thing. The problem was, porn and spam could be clicked away immediately, which made it possible to handle five hundred tickets a day. Now that we were stuck exclusively with the trickier tickets, our motivation was plummeting along with our scores: "My rating was below eighty *again*," Robert now said, and Sigrid, my sweet Sigrid, tried to calm him down. "I'll bring you some valerian tomorrow," she promised. "You can put drops of it in your tea." I still don't quite understand why I didn't just nod and give Robert a pat on the back like Kyo and Louis did, but no. Instead, I winked at him and said, "Don't feel obliged to take that stuff, okay?" and Sigrid suddenly looked so furious that for the rest of the break I didn't dare meet her eyes.

"Why aren't you saying anything?" I asked her on the bus.

"Because you'll just undermine me," Sigrid hissed back.

Lack of sleep, I told myself the couple of times that Sigrid gave me the silent treatment. She was just a little tired, we both were—yes, that's what I kept telling myself during those weeks, and it wasn't even that far-fetched. Sigrid was a poor sleeper, I'd noticed that early on. Ever since our first night together, she wanted me to hold her in bed. But her body, too, was different from Yena's, longer, slimmer, somehow she didn't fit into my arms as easily; holding her meant that eventually my right arm would start tingling. To get the blood flowing again sometimes I'd have to roll over onto my back for a bit. As soon as I let go, Sigrid would start tossing and turning and punching her pillow—she just couldn't get comfortable, she said, and we ordered pillows filled with cherry stones, but that didn't help. Sometimes I'd think she was asleep, but then a sudden sigh would give away that she was awake after all. Or I'd have to pee at five a.m. and I'd shimmy over to the bottom of the bed so I could get out without waking her, and she'd say something like "Well, hello there," as if we were bumping into each other in the supermarket, and then we'd both laugh, a little too loudly. She, for her part, did her very best to let me sleep the night through. But sometimes she'd suddenly say something in her sleep—something unintelligible that she kept repeating, and I'd shake her arm to expel whatever it was she was seeing, drive it away. On those nights, we'd sit up in the dark and I'd hold her close until she was completely quiet again.

I never asked her what she dreamed about. I had some ideas. But they were all things I'd rather not think about either, at least not at night, with the lights off and our desks at Hexa miles away.

But of course one day she ended up telling me anyway.

. . .

We were in the sports bar and Sigrid had asked for a Long Island iced tea. It was clear Michelle hadn't made that drink very often—that night her concoctions were so strong that even the guys quit after two rounds. But Sigrid was on a collision course. It took some serious negotiating before I was able to persuade her to at least share that third cocktail with me. The moment we got home, she staggered toward the bathroom. I held back her hair and when she was done I gave her a kiss on the forehead. We sat like that for a while, on the bathroom floor. "Are you okay?" I asked, and Sigrid mumbled something but didn't look up, her head resting on my forearm. The longer we sat like that, the heavier her silence grew. It wasn't a frosty silence, more a *demanding* silence—a silence that wanted something from me. Yes, it was clear that Sigrid expected a different question than "Are you okay?" and when it became clear that I was too chickenshit to ask that question, she went ahead and volunteered the answer: "I wasn't feeling well this afternoon," she said. Oh boy, I thought, here we go.

"Why not?" I said in a barely audible mumble, and

I stared straight ahead, at the spatters in the toilet bowl, which had been less than pristine to begin with.

"I don't know," she said.

But I could tell that she *did* know, that she wanted me to help her across a threshold even though I would have preferred to go sit against the radiator with her, but that wasn't what Sigrid needed right now. "Did you . . ." I began, but I could barely get the words out of my mouth. "Did you see something today?"

Sigrid nodded.

"Was it . . . very bad?"

Sigrid tried to shrug and almost slid out of my arms.

"Not really," she said.

We were still on the floor, me sitting straight up, her half lying down. She must have had a view of the rolls of toilet paper stacked behind the toilet bowl, and I think that made it easier for her to keep talking somehow. That afternoon she'd seen a video of a boy, she said. Just a kid, no older than twelve, the walls of his room covered in posters of ice princesses. "Not a strip of white wall left," Sigrid said. She seemed to be smiling and for a moment I hoped what she was about to tell me wasn't going to be that big a deal. The boy aimed his phone at his foot, Sigrid continued. He put an X-Acto knife between his big toe and second toe, pressing the tip into the webbing in between, as if he was about to surgically separate them from each other. He was being pretty clumsy about it, holding his phone in one hand as he brought the blade down with the other. The moment Sigrid saw blood, she'd turned it off.

"Why?" I asked, because she really should have watched the whole thing—for all she knew, genitals might have made an appearance next, or abuse by a third party.

"I couldn't do it," Sigrid said, and she made a snorting noise. "That video reminded me of something."

Of what, baby?

I said it reluctantly. Asking that question was like closing your eyes and running into a field full of dog shit, because what was she going to say? All kinds of options flashed through my mind, images of ankles, wrists, and ponytails I thought I'd forgotten—I felt my neck prickling with sweat and I briefly thought I was going to throw up too. Why was my love doing this? We'd done such a good job of keeping this crap out of this house, and now all of a sudden Sigrid wanted to talk. It felt as if she wasn't just soiling the toilet bowl but the whole room. Yes, I think I felt like her words would leave dark streaks on the tiled walls, send raw sewage flowing back up the shower drain; something I'd been afraid of for weeks, a looming disaster that had been lurking in acai berries and meditation apps all this time, but that I'd managed to keep at bay with feigned indifference: Baby, stop, I thought now that the two of us were sitting on the cold bathroom floor. Just stop, *please.*

But Sigrid went on. "It reminded me of another child," she said, and I tightened my grip. "A girl," Sigrid said. "I saw her a few months ago, around Christmas."

This Christmas girl was a little older than the boy she'd seen that afternoon. Instead of a knife the girl had used a loose razor blade. At the start of the video she'd placed the blade horizontally onto the skin under her eyes and pressed down.

Step by step, Sigrid told me how this girl had mutilated herself, and with every step I wondered what our guidelines said about it. If it was a livestream, we weren't allowed to intervene: As long as the person's followers could theoretically still help them, you had to let them carry on. If the video is prerecorded and the person looks "clearly underage," you forward it to the child protection department at an office abroad before taking it down—

77

you have to take it down or you risk inspiring copycat behavior, unless the video is newsworthy, in which case you have to leave it up. If the person who uploaded the video is also the person injuring themselves, you have to click the "Self-Harm" category and the user will receive a list of mental health resources, numbers they can call in their country of residence. If the user is threatening suicide, intervention is only required if they mention a specific time and place and claim that the act will be happening in the next five days: threat of suicide? live or recorded? newsworthy? clearly underage?—those questions became a refrain that drowned out Sigrid's story, and it took me a moment before I registered what she said next.

"Did you just say you looked her up?"

"Yeah."

"That girl?"

"Yeah. Online, I mean."

Of course you know that writing material is not allowed on the floor, Mr. Stitic. We're not allowed to write anything down, we're not even allowed to carry a piece of paper. One time John had to hand in his roll of breath mints because what if he were to write something on the wrapper (with his invisible pen, I guess). But Sigrid had remembered the girl's name. That was pretty impressive, since she saw hundreds of names flash by every day, but Sigrid—my sweet, clever Sigrid—had come up with a mnemonic, that day around Christmas. Nona Morgan Lindell, that was the girl's name: No Mona Lisa, Morgan Freeman, chocolate (Lindt, you see?). Sigrid looked Nona's profile up at home that same December evening. The video had disappeared, and it was jarring, being confronted with her own work like that: Shit, Sigrid thought, they've taken it down. But of course *she*'d been the one who had done it, and now she couldn't be completely sure that this was the right profile. But the teenager in the pictures did look like the girl she'd seen in the video that morning. No other users were listed under "Family." She was smiling rather broadly in her profile picture, her skin had been digitally smoothed out, and she was wearing a headband with pink cat ears—yes, those were all popular teen trends at the time, but it all seemed to be laid on a little thick. The longer she spent looking at this profile, the more suspicious Sigrid became. Why wasn't this "Nona" tagged in anyone else's photos? Whoever was behind the account put up a new selfie of the girl every other day in which she pouted seductively at the camera, sometimes with whiskers. Her "Favorites" included a cartoon channel, a number of makeup brands, and fan pages for Ko-

rean boy bands: Sigrid thought it seemed more like a car-
icature of a teenager than an authentic user profile. On
reflection, the whole thing was clearly a sham—what was
a teenager even doing on this platform in the first place?
Everyone knew they had abandoned it ages ago in favor
of their own dance and lip-syncing apps. The profile was
fake, Sigrid decided. And the video with the razor blade
probably had been too—what exactly was it she'd seen?
Hadn't it been implausibly elegant, the way the blood
had run down the girl's cheeks? If only she could watch
it again. For the second time that winter's evening, Sigrid
cursed herself for having done her job.

"What an odd story, baby," I said. We were still sitting
on the bathroom floor, Sigrid a little more slumped than
before. Anyone seeing us like this would have thought
she was about to be sick again, but Sigrid barely seemed
aware of her uncomfortable position. Her silence told me
she wasn't finished.

"And then what?" I asked quietly. "What happened
then?"

"I went back," Sigrid said.

"To the girl?"

"To her profile, yeah."

That had been on January third, more than three weeks

after Sigrid had first seen Nona's video. Sigrid had the day off and she was tired and she was bored. No Mona Lisa, Morgan Freeman, chocolate—it turned out she still remembered. Part of her hoped the profile would be gone— fake accounts never lasted long. But it was still there. The same profile picture, the same content—with one major difference. Nona's page had been flooded with messages from classmates, teachers, neighbors, her track team. They all wrote that they were going to miss Nona, because she'd been such a special girl, a bit of an introvert, maybe, but very warm and friendly. Sigrid snapped her laptop shut and went to buy groceries, and despite how tired she was, she completely reorganized her closet that evening. It didn't help. That night she couldn't sleep, and not long after, the nightmares had begun.

And not long after that, she'd started hitting on me, I thought in a flash, and for a moment her persistence took on a new meaning, but I didn't say anything, and tucked Sigrid's hair behind her ears. We sat quietly on the floor for a while.

"That video wasn't live, right?" I finally asked.

"No," Sigrid said.

"And you forwarded it to Child Protection?"

Sigrid nodded.

"No indicators of suicide?"

Sigrid shook her head.

"Well, then you did what you could, baby, didn't you?"

Sigrid's bad dreams didn't stop after that evening with the Long Island iced teas. She still jolted awake every couple of nights, and each time I'd take her into my arms. "It's not your fault," I said at first, but Sigrid didn't seem to want to hear that, she growled in response to everything I said, which confirmed what I already knew deep down: Talking, endlessly dredging things up, is pointless, plain and simple. She started eating more leafy greens, brewed tea from bitter herbs, and amassed a collection of glass bottles in the fridge: "natural" supplements. "Who says that what you've read about it is worth more than what I've read about it?" she'd bite back when I cautiously expressed my doubts about their efficacy. She'd stopped offering me her miracle cures, but then again, I never asked. She wanted to go to bed earlier and earlier when she stayed over at my place. Her palpitations were due to a lack of sleep, she said; sometimes she'd be tucked up by seven thirty. I'll be honest—we barely had sex anymore.

I never told Dr. Ana any of this. Especially not what happened next. Right before the third session, I called her and canceled, and I canceled again the week after—she was a little too curious about me and Sigrid. But I suspect you will understand, Mr. Stitic. You know what things were like at Hexa, you know my colleagues, you know what our normal looked like. So let me explain what kept me going that summer.

One morning, Hexa sprang a bunch of house rules on us. Suddenly there were printouts everywhere on the walls and windows—from a distance they looked like lists of names, as if we were about to find out who'd been cast in the school play. It turned out to be a set of new office commandments, worded very succinctly. One: No alcohol in and around the building. Two: No drugs in and around the building. Three: No head coverings on the work floor. And then, all the way down at the bottom, number four: No sex acts in and around the building.

We all knew that was about the lactation room. A few days earlier, three people had been caught in the room for nursing mothers on the third floor, after which the lock had been taken off the door so that people couldn't shut themselves in there. However, before long that measure was reversed due to protestations from the workforce: I'd heard some girls complaining in the hallway that a lactation room without a lock on it was unlawful. So were these new house rules supposed to take care of the problem? Call it childish, but at the end of our afternoon shift Sigrid and I snuck down the stairs to the third floor to thoroughly investigate the situation. We weren't the only ones—a number of different voices could be heard coming out of the lactation room, and we bumped into John and a new girl in the hallway. Our mission evolved from objective reconnaissance into a quest for an empty room—and let me tell you, it wasn't easy: That night I ended up fingering Sigrid between the dumpsters behind the building.

"Sex acts in and around the building." For us it was the first time, and it *worked*, much better than when we were at home and Sigrid wanted to drink tea and go to bed—it was a breath of fresh air, to tell you the truth. Of course, after that we wanted more, and a few days later we discovered a kind of supply closet, a small room crammed with boxes and objects that it took us a few times in there to realize were the parts of a disassembled copy machine.

Sigrid went and stood against the only empty wall, and I went down on her.

The supply closet became our regular spot, and no one caught us in there. Kind of a shame, I thought after the first few times. I began to wonder what would happen if someone walked in on us going at it between the photocopier parts, and sometimes I'd get myself off to that thought at home when Sigrid was already in bed.

There was an elevator, but it wasn't meant for us. You needed a pass, and we lowly moderators from the fifth floor didn't have one. That pass became a holy grail for me and Sigrid—we asked Jaymie if he maybe had one, and when he wanted to know why, we giggled like teenagers. Soon after that we came up with a plan. Half an hour before the start of our shift, Sigrid and I took up position in the hallway. We pretended we were looking at something on my phone, until we saw a man heading for the elevator. "Wait up," Sigrid called out, "we're going up to the tenth floor!"—for a moment, once again I was very proud of her. This guy was for real carrying a leather briefcase, as if he was trying to distinguish himself from the riffraff on the fifth floor, and we saw him hesitate, but of course he couldn't say no to two respectable-looking women, so there we were: the three of us crowded into a five-by-seven-foot box. Part of me felt like slipping my hand under Sigrid's shirt there and then, right in front of him, because for a split second I saw us through his eyes: two women getting it on, one of them not even that hot, shock, horror—somehow I found it incredibly exciting that his revulsion might turn him on even more (and give him a scandalous hard-on before our very eyes). The man got off the elevator on the eighth floor, and as soon as the doors closed I pushed Sigrid up against the control panel and put my hand between her legs, but no, she wasn't going to be wet before we reached the tenth. Too bad, I thought to myself.

Not enough time, apparently.

It was during this time that the last few people transferred the contents of their hip flasks into discreet plastic bottles, and by July pot use was at an all-time high. One day Sigrid even brought her own canned cocktails. That was new— before she'd only drunk and smoked what others had offered her. But those drinks—cheap gin and tonic, and sickly sweet rum and Coke that Souhaim called a threat to our taste buds—became a habit. I didn't say anything. Alcohol and chia seeds—it was a slightly odd combination but hey, it was her body, and I didn't feel like having any more arguments. Besides, things were going well, I thought—with me, with us: Wow, look at us! I remember thinking one afternoon. It's summer and here we are, on our wall, the sun on our pale faces, my arm around her beautiful waist—no, there wasn't much to be unhappy about; I had a job and I had friends and I was holding a beautiful woman and that was more than I'd ever dared dream of because, you know, many summers before I'd also spent my lunch breaks hanging around in a parking lot. Back then I'd sit leaning against other people's cars by myself: Hidden from the other girls' sight, I'd stare at the polka-dot pattern of chewing gum on old asphalt, hoping that Kitty from the eleventh grade wouldn't be coming up to me that day to call me a dyke—or worse, to sit down next to me and silently pinch my thigh. When I thought back to those days, I felt downright blessed, Mr. Stitic. Sure, the work we did was fucking awful but we could handle it, because we, Sigrid, the guys, and me, we were a team, and we'd get each other through it somehow.

Yes, that's what I believed, that summer.

/ / /

Are you familiar with the flat Earth theory, Mr. Stitic? We're not living on a ball but on a floating disk beneath a giant translucent dome. The sun, the moon, and the stars are all projections, and the CIA is jerking us around like we're extras on a Hollywood set: Flat Earthers, as the proponents of this theory call themselves, make up a sizable group of people—it's a movement of millions. They spread their ideas through message boards and chat groups—by now they have more than fifty-five million videos to their name: "So many it would take more than one lifetime to watch them all," I once heard a believer claim proudly.

I saw a lot of flat Earth material during my time at Hexa, you know. Users on the platform would often flag that stuff as offensive, but claiming that the Earth is flat (or that terrorist attacks were actually false-flag operations perpetrated by the government and lethal viruses were manufactured in labs) isn't against the rules. We still had to sit through the whole video every time, though, because for all we knew some weirdo had tried to debunk the basic principles of gravity by throwing a newborn baby out of a sixth-story window. If those videos went on for more than a few minutes, they'd start to get on my nerves, but the flat Earther memes made me laugh: pictures of NASA leaders as the Wizard of Oz or the Pied Piper, detailed diagrams about "Photoshop errors" in official photos of our planet —compared to other conspiracy communities, those flat Earth types seemed . . . kind of harmless, and well organized at that, with their own international conferences, T-shirts, and gadgets: "What is that?" I asked Kyo one afternoon, pointing at his wrist.

The four of us were standing at our bus stop; Louis smirked and started shaking his head. "It's a watch," Kyo said, holding it up for me and Sigrid to see. It took me a moment to understand what I was looking at. The dial was a map surrounded by a white ring—the fantasy world from some book, I thought, that seemed like the sort of thing Kyo might be into. Except the glass pane over the dial wasn't flat; it was slightly convex, like a tiny cloche. Or a dome.

"Flat Earth," Louis coughed unsubtly, and Kyo yanked his wrist back. "Hey," he mumbled, "don't look at me like that, Kayleigh," and Louis smirked again.

Apparently the others already knew about Kyo's new faith community, but somehow this development had passed me by, and I was genuinely taken aback.

"You think it's bullshit, don't you," Kyo said, and he sounded petulant, like an angry teenager falsely accused of knocking over a vase when actually it was the cat's fault.

"Sorry," I said, "but the Earth is round."

Kyo shook his head. "It's flat," he insisted, and Louis quipped that I was better off not asking any follow-up questions, but it was too late: "Why would the Earth be flat?"

"There's no proof that it's round."

"I believe there is."

"Okay, explain it to me then, would you?"

The thing was, though, I couldn't explain it. It had

been a long time since I'd last studied physics or geography, and to be honest, at this point I mainly knew arguments in favor of the notion that the Earth *wasn't* round, even though I'd never doubted that they were a load of shit.

"See?" Kyo said. "You can't. Meanwhile, the evidence that the Earth is flat is becoming impossible to deny."

"Why would the scientists lie to us?" I asked, but deep down I already knew the answer, and Kyo looked seriously angry now: "Because they've been doing that for ages. If they let the cat out of the bag now they'd lose all their credibility and, by extension, their status and their power over us."

"There are whistleblowers," I heard next to me. This was Sigrid, who was actually nodding along with Kyo. "There are scientists and professors who've confirmed that the Earth is flat, but if they took it to the mainstream media they'd lose their jobs." Sigrid was playing with the pull tab of her canned cocktail. She sounded completely calm, like she was just sharing some handy tips about how to hang a picture, no biggie.

"Yeah, but *guys*," I pleaded, "I've seen those videos too, okay? Except it really isn't true."

"You don't know that," Kyo said, after which I must

have thrown Louis a somewhat desperate look, because he suddenly raised his hands as if he was being held at gunpoint: *I'm not getting into this, friend.*

"There are no flights between—" Sigrid began.

"No," I interjected, "that's not true."

"You don't know what I—"

"I *do*. You were about to say that there are no direct flights between the continents in the Southern Hemisphere because the duration of those flights would give away what the map of the world really looks like, but there are plen—"

"Stop, you're not letting me finish!"

I'm sorry, I immediately thought. I need to apologize right away, tell Sigrid I'm sorry, because she doesn't like it when I undermine her in front of our friends, but then Kyo's bus pulled up and Louis started clapping him on the back by way of a manly goodbye. I quickly fist-bumped Kyo, and before he got on, he turned around one more time. "I get it," he said, sounding more paternal than angry all of a sudden. "We'll talk about it some other time. I used to be just like you."

As soon as Kyo's bus had driven off, Louis discreetly turned away from me and Sigrid—I was grateful to him for pulling his phone out of his back pocket.

"I'm sorry," I said to Sigrid. "I'm sorry for interrupting you."

"That's okay," she replied, sounding a little flat. And she took my hand and I squeezed but she didn't squeeze back, her hand lay limply in mine, and if I kept squeezing much longer I'd probably end up hurting her.

Not long after that, Sigrid went on vacation. Her ex had rented an apartment near the beach: "It's great for Mickey, he can run around all he wants." Although she claimed she'd been "toying with the idea" of going down there with Pete for a while, her announcement came as a surprise: She'd be leaving in early August and she'd be gone for at least two weeks.

"I really wouldn't make it any longer than that. What if you have a hard time getting back into it?"

"Back into what?"

"Work, the guidelines. What if you can't keep up anymore?"

Sigrid looked at me like she wasn't sure if I was serious. "I think it'll be fine."

She needed it, she said. She'd be able to clear her head

by the sea, maybe finally get a good night's sleep—didn't I understand she needed that? Oh yeah, I thought, and who's going to hold you at night? But I didn't want to be difficult. I wanted her to have that time away—honest, I did. I may have asked why she wasn't going away with *me* a few more times, but she kept saying it was just that Pete had asked her to come along first.

"Is Pete's new girlfriend coming too?"

"No, they broke up. Didn't I tell you?"

Every day she was gone, Sigrid sent me pictures, mainly of Mickey: the dog in the surf, the dog on a deck chair, a straw hat cocked on his head. The images made me smile every time, except when I could see Pete's thumb or a bit of his pant leg in the background. Meanwhile, I was feeling kind of restless at work. I missed our little excursions up to the supply closet, and my fingers, neck, shoulders, and wrist all hurt at night.

One afternoon I called Mehran, and that same evening he was sitting next to me on the sofa. We hadn't seen each other in months. The last time he'd been at my place I'd fed him some line about how I was working for the customer service department of a cable company. Now we were playing an old first-person shooter, a game we both knew really well. Maybe we were hoping the familiar game would help us fall back into our old dynamic; there were more awkward silences than there used to be—but it didn't help, the game.

"Can you turn down the volume?" I asked, startled because I'd said what I was thinking out loud.

"Why?" Mehran asked.

"It's too much," I said, and although he probably didn't understand, he let me turn the sound off. The rattle of machine gunfire, the reloading of Kalashnikovs, but especially the screams when characters got killed—suddenly they gave me a tight feeling in my chest that made me lose interest in the bowl of nachos on the floor.

I would much rather have played a racing game instead, but I knew that Mehran didn't like racing games. I also knew that he'd immediately set aside his loathing of them if I explained my objections, but I didn't. After all, I could already guess what he would say.

When we said goodbye that evening, Mehran hugged me a little longer than he usually did. I never called him again after that.

Now that I was all by myself, the muggy evenings passed agonizingly slowly. The heat didn't even help with my pain—the opposite, in fact, the stabbing sensation in my right shoulder kept getting worse. To distract myself a little, I decided to do something I hadn't done in a while: watch porn. Before Sigrid and I got together—i.e., when I was still home alone every now and then—I sometimes watched videos in which notionally gay women seduced notionally straight women: "College Girl Seduces Roommate," that kind of thing. Now that I was visiting my favorite porn site again for the first time in a while, the algorithm immediately served up new content that reflected my old preferences: "Masseuse Seduces Straight Client" or something along those lines. I clicked the title and saw a girl lying on a massage table. A slightly older blond woman came in carrying a stack of tiny towels and a bottle of massage oil—*Hi, how are you*—and then something strange happened to me. I started feeling agitated. My neck was bothering me and I felt the urge to get up, and not because what I was seeing was particularly offensive. If anything, it was because it suddenly struck me as so unbelievably *boring*. During my first few months at Hexa I'd seen hundreds of videos with women like these, but the moment they lay down on a massage table they'd immediately get about four dicks shoved in their face. The masseuse in the video I'd clicked just now, on the other hand, began to leisurely rub the panties of her "straight client." It was like I was watching a freaking nature documentary, or, no, something even more insipid than that: a video of a crackling fireplace. I fast-forwarded to the moment when the panties finally came off—not even that long ago, I would have found that incredibly exciting, but now I almost felt angry at how long it was taking.

I started searching for other genres that evening. And when I couldn't find what I was looking for, I traded my favorite porn website for an alternative search engine—the progressive kind that doesn't store your search terms.

I think I wasn't the only one who missed Sigrid. We suddenly saw a lot less of Kyo while she was gone. I think he was still offended by our skepticism vis-à-vis flat Earth, and now that Sigrid was sitting on the beach with man and dog, Souhaim, Louis, Robert, and I seemed to have lost our allure. More and more often, Kyo spent his breaks standing with a group of guys who Louis had once called "a bunch of nerds"—although at the time, all of us, Louis included, had sensed that wasn't exactly a scathing insult: With their brilliant-white designer sneakers and thick cotton polo shirts, those students, or whatever they were, undoubtedly wore the term "nerd" as a badge of honor. One afternoon they were standing just a few feet away from us, cackling. We saw Kyo gasping for breath with his hands on his knees as if he was choking on his own laughter. "Attention whores," Louis muttered, and I nodded, Robert gave a glassy stare, and I caught Souhaim shaking his head —not because he was annoyed by Kyo and his new crew; if anything, because he realized how low we'd fallen. Because just look at us: resentful of other people's fun, like someone's neurotic neighbor.

The way I remember it, that was the day Robert made his announcement. We were standing in the sports bar in the evening, and before we'd even touched our drinks, Robert said: "Guys, there's something I have to tell you." Despite the pot smell that came wafting off him, he seemed kind of nervous. I thought: Oh God, what if he's about to confess that he's in love with one of us or something? But instead Robert announced that he was going to leave us. "I can't handle working at Hexa anymore," he said, and his solemn enunciation told me he'd rehearsed his words. "I haven't been able to handle it for a long time." Before Robert had even finished, Souhaim and Louis leaned over him and the three of them briefly melted into a tangle of muscular limbs, the kind you normally only see on a soccer pitch after a goal or an irrevocable loss. "This is brave, man," Souhaim whispered, and now Robert shook his head. "I just don't feel like a *person* anymore."

"I understand," I said as I put my arms around him. I felt him shake his head against my neck. "No, sweet Kayleigh," he whispered. "You don't understand. You've got your own house, you've got options," and before I could reply, Souhaim grabbed Robert again. "You'll be all right, you hear me?" and I saw Louis close his eyes and sigh.

Robert's last shift was just two days later. Louis gave him a shot glass with his name on it, which he accepted with tears in his eyes; Louis was so adamant that it was nothing that I began to suspect it wasn't the first time he'd put together this parting gift, which briefly made me want to put my arms around *him*, too. Kyo also came to say goodbye to Robert. They clasped each other's right hands, hooked their fingers together, and for a moment it looked like they were arm-wrestling in midair. "Too bad Sigrid's not here," Kyo said, and everyone nodded and my stomach swelled with self-pity, because even though Sigrid would be back soon I suddenly felt like some kind of lonely widow, and that night I went at it like crazy, until my clit was raw and sore.

On the day of Sigrid's return, we were in the middle

of an official heat wave. The parking lot was in direct sunlight and we couldn't sit on our wall; the hot bricks would have branded our bare legs. During those days, the people who weren't smoking stayed inside, on our breaks we hung around in the downstairs lobby, it all felt kind of disjointed—it reminded me of that time Barbra and I spent eleven hours in a packed airport after a snowstorm had grounded all flights: Now, too, groups of people were sitting on the floor passing around slices of orange. Sigrid and I positioned ourselves against a wall. I would have preferred to go up to the supply closet with her right away, but we'd barely talked since she got back, so I asked her if she'd had a nice vacation.

"It was okay," she said casually.

"Yeah?"

"Yeah. It was nice to get away for a bit."

When I didn't immediately reply, she gave me a quick kiss on the cheek, and before I knew it, Kyo was standing in front of us telling Sigrid how much he'd missed her: "And did you know that Robert has left?"

That night Sigrid stayed over at my place like always. I hugged her close. She disentangled herself and I grabbed a hold of her again until she mumbled something like "Too hot."

• • •

As for what happened next, Mr. Stitic, opinions vary. That is to say, Sigrid's version differs considerably from mine, inasmuch as I even understand her version—she was pretty emotional the last time we talked. But if you put a gun to my head and said, *Tell me about your last weeks together, about what* really *happened between August fifteenth and thirtieth*, I'd tell you this: *As far as I'm concerned it wasn't that too* much *happened—if anything, too little.*

After Sigrid's return, we went back up to the supply closet a few more times, and on one occasion Sigrid even suggested we film ourselves. "So we can watch it together later," she said. Believe it or not, I was touched. I thought: Maybe she's trying to make it up to me (although as far as I was concerned there was no need, her being back from vacation was more than enough). And it was exciting, that third, digital eye trained on us, I remember it really got me going. We never got around to watching it after—but I had no reason to read into that.

Something, though, did change following that afternoon. More and more often Sigrid came up with an excuse to skip the third floor. She felt queasy after eating that tuna sandwich, she was tired, or she wanted to catch the first bus home because she was making vegetarian lasagna and she needed to soak the pasta sheets. I was bummed, but I wasn't that surprised. I often recalled something I'd once overheard Barbra telling an old friend of hers: "The more you get to know each other, the more awkward the sex becomes," and although I still think Barbra was talking about other people at the time—mutual friends from her book group or whatever—it was frighteningly accurate with regard to our relationship at that point. Okay then, I thought as I listened to Sigrid's story about that iffy tuna sandwich, apparently we've gotten to the next stage now —I saw her subtle rejections as proof of intimacy, you understand?

Sigrid had more or less moved back in with me at this point, and she talked a lot about the two of us going to stay in that apartment by the sea—she was sure Pete would be able to get us a discount. She even suggested introducing me to Pete—she'd already told us both so much about each other and he was curious about me, she said—so one afternoon we all went for a stroll around the lake on the edge of town with Mickey. In what I think was a mutually polite attempt to align our speeds, we walked painfully slowly, and Pete told us all about the bamboo farm he'd invested in.

During those days, Sigrid drank a lot less than she had before. She started sleeping a little better too. As for me, I slept a little worse now that we barely went up to the supply closet anymore, but I won't go so far as to say those two things were related. I will admit that I thought I was quite the gentleman for never waking her. On one or two occasions I got myself off next to her, just so I could get to sleep, and I assure you: If she'd done the same thing I would have considered that the most normal and logical thing in the world. So you can lower your gun, Mr. Stitic. This was what life was like during those days. We fantasized about a future together. About paying off debts in one go (me), studying nutritional science (her), adopting a Maltese puppy (her), living together for real (both of us), "finding an even better-paying job" (me), "you mean finding a *normal* job, honey" (her).

And yet Sigrid claims she experienced things differently. And by now my memories of our final weeks together, and maybe even of the weeks before, are like the chunk of iron pyrite on my Aunt Meredith's bookshelf. Under the most favorable circumstances it looks like a nugget of real gold, but when you turn down the lights the mineral turns a silvery blue, and when you stand right in front of it at night, you're looking at a black, seemingly charred lump of coal.

All right, on to the next question. What happened on August 30, the day Sigrid left me? That one's a little trickier. Sometimes I think I understand it, but before long I'm back to overanalyzing what she said, what I said, what we did and didn't do in the run-up to that day, and then I start doubting again: Maybe it was different. And briefly that idea, the notion of an alternative, mitigating explanation, lifts the anvil off my stomach, but after a few free breaths it comes crashing back down into place—because I recall Sigrid's final words, for example.

In short, my memories of that second-to-last August day can be explained in a number of different ways. So first let me tell you what exactly was done and said that Friday.

It's twenty past two when I walk into the parking lot. The scorching heat of the previous few weeks has given way to a generous late-summer sun, and all of a sudden I'm looking forward to fall: My chest tingles at the thought of plaid scarves and galoshes, squirrels, gathering pinecones—I don't have much experience with any of those things, but it's what I was taught about fall in elementary school and I haven't been able to curb my desire for pinecones since, every September it rears its head anew—I find myself feeling strangely cheerful, and a touch melancholy.

Then I see: Sigrid is standing with Kyo today, right in the middle of the parking lot, with Kyo and two guys from his new crew. They're kind of gawky, one is wearing a gray baseball cap and the other a bulky, wrinkle-free rain-coat—it appears they're not immune to that autumn feeling either. What must have happened, I think to myself, is that Kyo went up to my girl and then Cap and Coat joined them. Maybe it's time I did the polite thing and introduced myself to them (I told you I was in a good mood, didn't I?). But then I see Louis sitting on our wall by himself. He sees me too and raises a hand in a gesture that is more question than expectation, and apparently I'm not that eager to hang out with Cap and Coat after all, because I tell myself: I'll see Sigrid soon enough. I remain loyal to our wall and sit down next to Louis; he claps me on the back and we clear our throats and say, "Hey, man, how's it going?"

Except Sigrid doesn't come. She's still over there with Kyo, and I see her asking his new friends for a light.

Before long Louis and I have run out of things to say. Having a direct view of Kyo and Sigrid reduces us to spectators, which only makes us quieter. "D'you wanna . . ."

" . . . go over there for a minute?" Louis adds, and we nod and get up off the wall.

"Oh, hi!" Sigrid says when she sees us. She sounds like she wasn't expecting us, like we're two acquaintances from her salsa dancing class who she only invited out of politeness and, shit, now suddenly we're the first guests to arrive at her party. She introduces us to Cap and Coat, but I immediately forget their names, because something is going on. The guys glance over at Louis and exchange a look I can't read, which prompts Louis to ask: "Are we interrupting something?"

"Of course not," Sigrid says, and then she does something I'll continue to hold against her for a long time: She answers the question. Truthfully. "We were talking about Soros," she says, and I can tell she's trying to sound as casual as possible: Nothing to see here, they were just talking about Soros, George Soros, the richest Jew in the world, and by extension the most hated Jew in the world—oh yeah, there's that. Suddenly everyone is looking at Louis: Kyo, Sigrid, Cap, Coat, and even me, although of course that's fucking stupid. But Louis stays calm, he just smirks.

"Ah," he says, "Soros, our good old philanthropist. If it were up to him, we'd be ankle-deep in raw sewage from refugee camps, am I right?"

I detect sarcasm, but Cap and Coat elbow each other in the ribs like they can't believe what they're hearing: The only Jew they know is attacking the most famous Jew in the world.

"It's true, though," Kyo says. And he sounds stern, because he knows Louis, knows he's being facetious. "If that guy goes on like this, they'll end up running this place," Kyo says, "and no one's doing anything about it."

"It's an outrage," Louis says, and now even Cap and Coat's poorly tuned antennas are picking up on his derision.

"I wouldn't be so dismissive if I were you," Cap says.

"Don't tell me you don't know what Soros is doing," Coat chimes in.

"I know what Soros 'is doing,'" Louis says, making air quotes. "I've been working here a little longer than you, girls."

He's about to turn around, but then Cap says: "That sob story about his parents during the war isn't true, you know," and Coat nods: "That whole Holocaust probably never happened."

Louis stops in his tracks. He looks at them as if they've just thrown a pebble down the front of his shirt—more incredulous than angry. "Give me a break," he says. "I thought you guys were smarter than that," and again Louis tries to walk away, but Coat doubles down: "It's true, though, isn't it? That's how powerful Soros is. Who do you think is bankrolling the biggest lie in history?"

The biggest lie in history—I'd heard that line before. That's how the videos begin that "explain" step by step that there's hardly any proof of the existence of gas chambers during the Second World War. That Jews in internment camps only died of infectious diseases, diseases that were treated with Zyklon B, the gas that was later found on their clothes: "a completely harmless pesticide." We're only allowed to take those videos down if they've been uploaded in a country where Holocaust denial is criminalized, and where the local authorities actively prosecute offenders: *Germany, France, Israel, and some weird place like Australia,* I sum up in my head, while right in front of me, in broad daylight, a pretty fatal collision is taking place.

"How many Jews died in the Second World War? Four hundred thousand at the most," Coat barrels on, and Cap tries to overtake him: "Compared to twenty million Russian soldiers," he says, and then Coat goes ahead and floors the gas pedal: "Ever heard of the Haavara Agreement? The Nazis and the Jews worked together to justify the annexation of Israel."

Louis is remarkably quiet all this time. He clears his throat pointedly and then nods at Kyo: "Hey, do you believe this stuff too?" Kyo looks at me, and then at Sigrid, and then at his own hands. He doesn't look at Louis when he says, "Well, the part with the gas chambers isn't very plausible."

"It's not?" Louis asks, and he sounds more pleading than angry. I think back to how he waved at me earlier and suddenly I understand what's at stake for him. "And how about the fact that they exterminated my grandpa's favorite uncle? Is that not very plausible either?"

Cap and Coat are nudging each other now: "My grandpa's favorite uncle," they find that funny because it sounds so gay—I'm sure Louis hears them chuckling, but he only looks at Kyo, the one he loves the most and who therefore is committing the greatest betrayal.

Kyo is still staring at his hands. "I don't know." And then, suddenly, Louis smirks again. He gives a curt nod.

And then he plows straight into Kyo: "What's wrong with you, man? What are you jerking off these fascists for? What kind of inferiority complex do you have that you need to suck up to the freaking Ku Klux Klan over here? You're practically a chink yourself, for fuck's sake! Jesus Christ, Kyo, who knew, you don't just look like a fat pig, you also have ground pork for brains—hey, have you told your new fuck-buddies that the Earth is flat?"

"Well, actually . . ." Coat mumbles, but Louis doesn't hear him: "Well? Where's your jewelry, you little faggot?"

I only notice now that Kyo is no longer wearing his flat Earth watch. He's just standing there, shaking his head like he doesn't know what to do: save his reputation with Cap and Coat or punch Louis in the face, and then, then Sigrid intervenes. "Okay, guys," she says, "that's enough now"—God, I love her so much it makes me weak in the knees. Because that's my girl, that's my Sigrid: After a bad start, now she seems to be the one who's taken charge of the race. "Yeah, guys," I say, "she's right, that's enough!"

For a moment it seems like that's defused the tension. The guys are already looking at each other: Is it time to clap each other on the back like brothers? But then Sigrid pipes up again. "There's something to be said for both sides," she declares solemnly, and I look at her.

There she is, my Sigrid, her hands shoved in the pockets of her slightly too thin summer pants, her hair pulled

up in a high ponytail. If I grabbed her now, I'd smell cigarettes and the appley scent of her favorite perfume: a smell
I don't like but that turns me on anyway, yes, there she
is, Sigrid, my girlfriend, I know what she looks like when
she comes, I could draw a map of the stretch marks on
her butt, I know the names of her childhood pets, I know
her favorite seat on the bus and her ideal sleeping position. I've heard her cry and seen her throw up, I'm allowed
in the bathroom when she's doing her makeup or when
she's peeing, I know that she finds a made bed unsexy and
I know the look that tells me she secretly disagrees with
something. She's even told me what keeps her up at night,
and that makes me feel like I know her. But maybe I'm
wrong, maybe I don't know her at all. That idea makes
me anxious, I need to check if it's true, *I need to verify it* —
maybe it's this thought that makes me do what I do next,
ask what I'm asking: "I'm sorry, *what?*"

"I'm just saying—" Sigrid begins, but it's already too
late, I don't want to hear it anymore. And I can feel things
going wrong, I know I should keep my mouth shut—I'm
even apologizing in my head, because once again I'm talking over her but I can't help myself, I feel like a goose being
force-fed bullshit through a metal tube, yes, I've been
stuffed so full of stupidity that something needs to come

out, a violent, irrepressible belch: "Only *complete idiots* believe the Holocaust doesn't exist!"

Even Louis looks startled now. He's not looking at me, but at Sigrid: How is she going to respond to such an affront—and from her own girlfriend, no less? Then the guys all start talking at once: Cap is talking over Coat, and Louis is shouting all kinds of things at Kyo—they can't possibly be hearing each other, arguments are lost in the cacophony of pointed accusations and random insults—it's almost as if the guys are doing it on purpose, as if they're trying to help me by putting up a wall of noise to separate me from Sigrid, shield us from the inevitable.

"Fuck you," Sigrid snarls. And she comes up to me and whispers in my ear, a move she must have seen in a movie: "We're finished, Kayleigh."

Sigrid marches off and the guys fall silent. The way I remember it, the five of us watch her go—yes, in my mind's eye I can see us all standing there: me at the front, Louis and Kyo flanking me like bodyguards, with Cap and Coat right behind me so that I can't fall, can't buckle under the loss.

I won't see or talk to Sigrid for the rest of the day. She must have gotten her phone from her locker and headed straight for the bus stop, three hours before the end of her shift. I'll call her but she won't answer, not that night, not the next day; I'm startled when I find out she's canceled her shifts for that weekend.

Okay, I'd offended Sigrid, I knew that. And I hadn't just offended her: I'd *undermined* her in front of other people—she hated that, and fair enough. I couldn't deny that it was stupid of me, but her reaction seemed, how can I put it, rather disproportionate. It almost felt like Sigrid had been trying to provoke me: She had been the one to bring up Soros, and she knew I didn't believe in all that conspiracy crap. Besides, the confrontation with Kyo had pretty much followed the same course as our flat Earth discussion previously. Sigrid should have known it was going to end like this—or was that what she'd been hoping would happen? Maybe, I thought during the days that followed, it was a test. Maybe I'd walked into a trap: Maybe Sigrid wanted to know whether I'd be able to control myself this time. Apparently not, she knew that now, but surely that was no reason to blow off work. So what was going on, what was I missing?

Maybe it was Kyo, I thought. It was obvious that he liked Sigrid. She must have been flattered by his adoration, maybe she didn't want to hurt him. Yes, maybe she felt bad about not reciprocating his feelings, and her sense of guilt had twice compelled her to say some very strange things—but then why had she gotten so mad at *me?* Her reaction to our altercation seemed impossible to justify. I had to find out through Souhaim that she'd started working the night shift—my God, the night shift, for someone with her sleep problems?

It was madness, Mr. Stitic. And before I go on, I want to ask you what you would have done. What would you do if the woman you love started completely ignoring you overnight? Not because you cheated or because you pushed her cat out the window, no, things are fine, really; just yesterday she made you eggplant casserole and today you disagreed with her at a party, that's all, and you want to apologize but you don't get the chance because your beloved has disappeared—poof!—from your life. Some of her clothes are still on the chair in your bedroom; there's a jacket and a scarf on the coatrack in the hallway. There's still water in the pan your beloved used to boil an egg this morning; she accidentally took your phone charger. So you call. You send a text to ask what's going

on. And then you send another text, and then—admit it
—another, if only to ask for your charger back. Maybe by
this point you go ahead and try to call again. Maybe you
call a few more times, and the next day you call again,
right? And you probably ask one or maybe several mutual
friends if by any chance they've seen her—admit it, you'd
do all of that, wouldn't you? But what if it doesn't get you
anywhere? What if nine more days go by during which
your beloved refuses any form of contact? You feel guilty,
you want to tell her you're sorry, you're frustrated, you're
angry, and oh, you're worried, that too. After all, this kind
of behavior is completely unlike her—maybe someone is
putting her up to it. Or maybe your beloved has—to put it
bluntly—gone crazy. Maybe she's succumbed to stress or
lack of sleep, for all you know she could be raving in the
street right now, hearing voices in her head. Either way,
you want to help her, but to be able to do that you first
need to know what's going on. So, Mr. Stitic, what would
you have done in this situation?

I bet you would have done the same as me. Just like
me, you would have waited for your beloved in the parking lot outside her office, am I right?

· · ·

I tried it on Sunday evening. Sigrid had failed to show up again that day and I suspected she was, indeed, working the night shift, she seemed to be in cahoots with the schedulers: Whenever I wasn't working they had her come in. I was one of the last people to leave that afternoon. Once I was outside I sat down on our wall, out of habit but also because from there I had a good view of who was coming and going. The first people working the night shift came straggling across the parking lot—they had come in cars. Around six thirty the first bus arrived, ejecting a group of people that moved toward the door in a huddle—look, there was Souhaim: I immediately sat up straight but I didn't recognize anyone else.

The evening crew didn't get paid more than those of us who worked the day shift. They were people who had a different job during the day, or people like Souhaim who didn't care when they were scheduled, maybe because they couldn't sleep at night anyway. The sun had set and I zipped up my coat; parked cars lost their shape to the darkness.

It was jarring seeing the familiar parking lot all grayed out, strange faces walking my regular route, a parallel world—had Sigrid been swallowed up by this alternate universe? She wasn't the only woman working the night shift. I saw others walking past, talking on the phone, sometimes with several bags hanging off one wrist, I imagined the marks those bags would leave and suddenly I thought I saw Sigrid, a slim figure in a leather jacket. She was walking quickly; I wasn't sure if it was her. This doubt would lead me to stay for the rest of the evening.

Time passed: eight p.m, nine p.m. I walked circles around the building, but I didn't dare venture too far. What if Sigrid came out during the break? What if one of those glowing cigarette tips belonged to her? I played a couple of games on my phone, getting rid of blocks and shooting balloons. I sat down in front of our wall instead of on it so that I had some back support. I did jumping jacks to stave off the cold, all the while keeping an eye on the windows of the fifth floor. From time to time I would see a silhouette—was that her? No, I'd decide, my Sigrid was slimmer, taller, her shoulders were broader, and part of me was proud that I found it so easy to pick out the impostors this time, as if it was a testament to how much I cared about Sigrid and, by extension, justified what I was doing.

Around one thirty in the morning, the first workers came trickling out of the building. I went and stood next to the sliding doors, not very inconspicuously—it was easier to see the faces in the light from the lobby. When Souhaim came out I was startled and looked down at the ground, hoping he wouldn't notice me. One by one our colleagues from the night shift came shuffling out into the parking lot, no one talking: When the woman in the leather jacket emerged my heart started racing even though I could see almost immediately that it wasn't Sigrid. After about forty-five minutes the flow of people came to a halt and the adrenaline ebbed from my body. She wasn't there. But, I thought, maybe she'd be there tomorrow: After all, I was off—if Sigrid was, in fact, actively avoiding me, she would have had them schedule her for a shift.

I did the math—it would be another five hours before the first of the morning crew arrived. The building was still open, maybe I could sleep in the supply closet if I moved some of the junk aside. I could sneak in, run up the stairs, but before I'd made up my mind a security guard came out to lock the sliding doors with a tiny key, like one for a padlocked diary. There I was, alone in the pitch-black parking lot. Shivering, I walked over to our wall. Could I fit behind there? I lay down, feeling the rough pavement through my coat, and pulled up one leg—that's how I slept in bed, too. The ground was cold and hard but the low wall offered shelter; I seemed to be shielded from the wind here, and the darkness calmed me—I've always felt protected by the dark, like it swallows up the monsters instead of hiding them. I closed my eyes and imagined staying there until the sun came up. I could have, I thought in the taxi home.

The next day I again positioned myself by the wall at five thirty. I sat down in front of it like I'd done the night before, and this time I'd come prepared: I'd brought bananas and a scarf that had been my mother's—unnecessarily, it turned out, because only an hour later Sigrid showed up. The muscles in my chest clenched when I saw her. So she really had changed shifts to avoid me.

I headed over to her and I saw her flinch. "Shit," she said out loud, and she froze, in the middle of the parking lot. I raised my hand in greeting and moments later we were standing across from each other silently. Sigrid nodded toward the office tower, like a drug dealer trying to stay out of the cops' line of sight, and began walking in that direction.

"What are you doing?" she asked. Now we were

standing right next to the building, not far from the spot by the door where I'd kept watch the previous night.

"Why are you so angry?" I asked.

"Because this is kind of intimidating," Sigrid said, and she glanced around as if she was about to press a tiny envelope into my hand: "You're stalking me, you're calling me thirty times a day," she hissed. Her answer confused me. "That's not what I mean," I said. "I meant: Why are you avoiding me?"

"Oh," Sigrid said, and nodded vehemently: "So you admit that you're stalking me? Souhaim told me you were here last night, too."

"Yeah, I was looking for you. I want to talk to you."

"Then why didn't you just ask to see me?"

"Because you're ignoring my messages."

"You don't know that."

"What?"

"You don't know that I would've ignored you if you'd asked me that."

Sigrid was being impossible, Mr. Stitic. And it didn't make me mad, it scared me, because Sigrid, my lovely, empathic Sigrid, was just standing there, her arms crossed; the whole situation reminded me vaguely of high school, all the times when Kitty and Shanice would take my bag or my skateboard off me and I confronted them with a teacher by my side: "Jeez, why didn't you just *ask* for it back?" Back then my sense of impotence filled me with a wild rage that made me want to grab the chunk of rose quartz on Kitty's necklace and ram it down her throat, but now that Sigrid was being similarly unreasonable, I mainly felt panicked. For a wild moment I suspected I'd walked into a trap, that my whole relationship with Sigrid had been some sort of joke, a bet with the guys, maybe, that she'd made the first time they saw me walking toward the wall: Let's see if we can make her believe she's pretty.

Sigrid lowered her arms. "Okay," she said in a tone I couldn't read—was she trying to get me upset? "So talk."

"I'm sorry," I said hurriedly.

"What exactly are you sorry about?" Sigrid asked, and I thought that was kind of a weird question, though I didn't change course accordingly—like when you notice that shrimp tastes funny but you're already swallowing it, that's how I said, "I'm sorry I got so worked up when you . . . implied that stuff about the Holocaust." I tried to phrase it as diplomatically as possible, but on the word "Holocaust" Sigrid started shaking her head. "You don't get it, do you?" she said. "You really don't get it."

I was taken aback by what Sigrid said next. Or, no, I'll

be honest, I was crushed. She must have noticed that I was thrown, to say the least, and a few days later she'd send me an email to explain things in some more detail—whether to kick me when I was down or help me understand, I don't know, I deleted her message immediately, hit *delete* with the fervor of someone trying to scrub a period stain out of her pants. And when I think back to our last conversation, over there, by the entrance of our shared workplace, I can't tell where the memories of that conversation overlap, intersect with, or get overtaken by my memories of that email—anyway, I'm avoiding the point.

What Sigrid claimed was this.

She didn't always want the same things as me. She'd tried telling me that, but I didn't listen. I kept crossing her boundaries. What's more, I didn't trust her—I was completely paranoid. Yes, I'd frightened her. How was she supposed to know how to break it off with me?

You were so overbearing, you acted like you knew everything.

Pete was really freaked out by the things I told him about you.

Didn't I tell you "I don't feel like having sex right now"? And then you'd touch yourself, right next to me.

Just look, Kayleigh, will you just look at the screen!

. . .

"Secondary trauma caused by long-term exposure to shocking images can cause depression, anxiety, and paranoid thoughts"—isn't that what it said in your press release? I have no doubt that it's true, but when I think about me and Sigrid I'm not sure which one of us was having the paranoid thoughts, although I would say I was being very trusting when, one Thursday afternoon, I let her prop up her phone in the left-hand shelving unit in the supply closet.

"That was a great idea," I remember saying afterward.

That doesn't exactly suggest a *lack* of trust, does it? If anything, I think it was incredibly naïve, because when we were standing in front of our office building that last time, Sigrid pulled her phone out of her pocket.

"Just look, Kayleigh, will you just look at the screen!"

"What is that?"

"This is us."

I looked, but I had a hard time making out the shadowy figures through the reflections on the glass. Sigrid turned up the volume and zoomed in using her thumb and forefinger.

"Tell me what you see."

"What you said: I see you and me."

"And does this look normal to you?"

"I don't see anything strange."

"Really? Listen to what I'm saying."

Sigrid pushed the phone against my ear.

"Stop, I can't hear."

"Jesus, Kayleigh."

Sigrid lowered her phone and restarted the video.

"Imagine this is a ticket. You see this at work—what do you do: Leave it up or take it down?"

"Oh, come on."

"No, I'm serious: This is a ticket. What do you see?"

"I don't see anything."

"Say it."

"Sexual content," I said quietly. "No female areola, no genitalia, so leave it up."

"Oh yeah? And what about this?"

Now Sigrid pointed at something on the screen.

"Erotic asphyxiation, no visible bruises or injuries, so: Leave it up."

"What about coercion?"

"No coercion. Leave it up."

"Come on, Kayleigh, listen to what I'm saying, just listen!"

Sigrid was about to push the cold device against my ear again, but right at that moment Souhaim and Louis came walking out of the building. I suspect they'd been walking right behind Sigrid earlier but had hidden in the lobby as soon as they saw that I was approaching, out of concern or morbid curiosity—I still hope it was the latter.

"Everything okay over here?" Souhaim asked. I expected Sigrid to lower her phone but she didn't. Instead she handed it to Louis: "If this was a ticket," she said, "would you guys leave this post up?"

Souhaim and Louis pored over the screen. "What is the one on the left saying?" Souhaim asked. "I can see her shaking her head no, but what is she saying?" and he was about to lift the phone up to his ear when Louis grabbed his arm. "What the fuck, you guys? That's you!"

I'd already turned around by that point. For the last time, I crossed the parking lot. I pulled up the hood of my sweatshirt and pretended I couldn't hear Sigrid's shouting.

/ / /

In the days that followed that last evening in the parking lot, I felt so ashamed that sometimes, out of nowhere, I'd hit myself in the face. I'd be watching a movie about race car drivers stuck in some dicey situation, my thoughts would wander to what had happened, and—*thwack!*—I'd have a red mark on my cheek. Or I'd try watching some porn, like a fucking idiot: *thwack! thwack! thwack!* at pretty much everything I saw. I set my alarm a few times with the intention of going back to Hexa, but I never did.

I never saw or spoke to Sigrid again, nor Souhaim, Robert, Louis, or Kyo. And yet for quite some time I held out the hope that things would be okay. That Sigrid and I would run into each other again, become friends, and, who knows, maybe go back to being more than that.

I'd even come up with a whole plan, Mr. Stitic.

No Mona Lisa, Morgan Freeman, chocolate.

Nona's parents' house was a four-hour drive in Aunt Meredith's old Buick (by this point I'd told her what kind of work I'd spent the past few months doing, although I lied about why I'd quit—I couldn't handle it anymore, I said, and without asking any more questions she lent me her car for a long weekend by the beach; "I'll be able to clear my head by the sea"—yeah, right).

It was a detached house on a plot of land just outside a medium-size city; Nona's childhood must have been full of tadpoles and pony rides. I drove a little way past the house and parked my car on the side of the road; I pictured Nona taking the bus to the center of town on Friday nights and wondered if she'd been charmed by the cloying pineapple cocktails and slimy boys' tongues that she'd undoubtedly encountered there.

It was a weekday in late September, six p.m.; I assumed Nona's parents were home. In the car, I'd rehearsed what I was going to say. I was a friend of someone who'd seen one of Nona's last videos (not as a moderator, of course, just as a normal person). My good friend didn't know what to do when she saw Nona like that, she didn't intervene, and now it was keeping her up at night—was there anything they would like me to tell her? For example, that it wasn't her fault? Maybe they'd find my question inappropriate. Worst-case scenario, Nona's parents would kick me out; in the best-case scenario, however, they would grant my "good friend" forgiveness, absolution, which I would then pass on to her over a cappuccino while holding her hand, maybe in the form of a note signed by both parents. And even if Sigrid pulled back her hand, at least she'd appreciate my gesture, she'd realize how noble my intentions were.

The hallway light was on. I rang the doorbell but nothing happened. I rang again: nothing, no noise, no surprised muttering. I stepped into the front yard to peer through the living room window: The beige curtains were closed and the light inside seemed to be coming from a single dim source—a desk lamp to deter burglars, I suspected. I walked around the house, noticed the lawn seemed unkempt; maybe Nona's parents were on vacation. Or maybe they preferred to mourn with family, maybe they couldn't stand being in their own environment—yes, that had to be it: Of course they still saw Nona sitting there when they looked at that swing in the backyard, still heard her laughter ringing through the sunroom. . . Hey, I thought, I wonder if that's her bedroom window?

Both the front door and the door to the sunroom were locked. But there was one other door on the right side of the building, green film, rotted wood. I jiggled the door handle and kicked the bottom of the door and what do you know—it flew open with a creaky squeal that, if the door hadn't been a door, could have expressed either surprise or indignation.

Suddenly I was in a small anteroom that led to a kitchen with a breakfast bar covered with silver candlesticks. I'd seen those before—the online furniture store that I'd answered the phones for sold them, and I knew they were more expensive than they looked.

The stairwell was lined with framed photographs. Nona as a baby on a stylish wooden changing table, Nona as a happy toddler playing on the beach, a slightly older Nona clambering onto a camel. They were nice pictures —good lighting, but not posed; maybe her parents had a knack for photographic timing, or maybe Nona was a girl who knew when to look away in order to look like herself. The further I climbed up the stairs, the fewer frames there were on the wall; evidently her parents had left some space for the pictures of Nona that hadn't been taken yet, and the knowledge that those pictures were never *going* to be taken suddenly lent those patches of white wall a solemn quality, the visual equivalent of a minute's silence—I almost didn't have the nerve to pant as I walked up past them.

There were four doors upstairs. The first one opened onto a bathroom, the second led into Nona's bedroom. I turned the light on. There were no flowers or cards on Nona's bed; in fact, the bright blue duvet was thrown haphazardly aside—evidently her parents were preserving this room in exactly the state they'd found it in that one terrible day. I went over to the desk that ran along the right wall. Nona had put picture frames on it. Hers were a lot more colorful than her parents': a purple one designed to resemble the frame of an antique painting, two others made of pink faux fur, and one with butterflies in relief encased photos of Nona with friends—I saw stuck-out tongues and flushed cheeks and one picture of Nona, a lot skinnier than in the other pictures, posing by herself in front of the castle in an amusement park. I picked up the frame, the one with the butterflies, and held it up right in front of my face. And what kinds of things did I see?

Nona was smiling with her lips pressed together, very different from the pictures in the stairwell. Her somewhat grown-up pose contrasted with the cheerful background, the pink turrets that almost seemed to be coming out of the back of her head. She was wearing a skirt and a tight top that exposed a flat tummy. Were those scratches on her arms, weren't her knees alarmingly bony? I went over to the window to look at the picture in daylight; the quality wasn't great, it must've been taken on a cell phone and then blown up—I could make out a few pixels here and there.

I heard keys jangling downstairs. Footsteps in the hallway, a tired female voice and a man's soothing words, and suddenly I saw myself standing there, like in the grainy footage of a security camera. Look, there I was, in Nona's bedroom, by the window, her portrait, her hollow cheeks and pale teenage wrists right next to my face, and I remember thinking: What the hell am I doing?

Leabharlanna Poiblí Chathair Baile Átha Cliath
Dublin City Public Libraries

SELECTED SOURCES

This novella is a work of fiction. The characters portrayed are drawn from my imagination. However, any resemblance to reality is not accidental. During my research into the working conditions of commercial content moderators worldwide, I made grateful use of the books, studies, documentaries, and articles listed below, which I recommend strongly to anyone interested in learning more about this topic. The sources, as listed below, pertain to the articles as they were on the date of publication.

Block, Hans, and Moritz Riesewieck, directors. *The Cleaners.* Cologne: Gebrueder Beetz Filmproduktion, 2018.

Cassidy, Ciaran, and Adrian Chen, directors. *The Moderators.* New York: Field of Vision, 2017.

Charon, Sjarrel de. *De achterkant van Facebook: 8 maanden in de hel* ("The Back End of Facebook: Eight Months in Hell"). Amsterdam: Prometheus, 2019.

Chen, Adrian. "The Laborers Who Keep Dick Pics and Beheadings Out of Your Facebook Feed." *Wired,* October 23, 2014, https://www.wired.com/2014/10/content-moderation.

Cox, Joseph, and Jason Koebler. "Content Moderator Sues Facebook, Says Job Gave Her PTSD." *VICE,* September 14, 2018, https://www.vice.com/en/article/zm5mw5/facebook-content-moderation-lawsuit-ptsd.

Duin, Maartje, et al. "De hel achter de façade van Facebook" ("The Hell Behind Facebook's Facade"). *De Volkskrant,* April 21, 2018, https://www.volkskrant.nl/nieuws-achtergrond/de-hel-achter-de-facade-van-facebook~b884f37c5.

Gilbert, David. "Bestiality, Stabbings, and Child Porn: Why Facebook Moderators Are Suing the Company for Trauma." *VICE,* December 3, 2019, https://www.vice.com/en/article/a35xk5/facebook-moderators-are-suing-for-trauma-ptsd.

Gillespie, Tarleton. *Custodians of the Internet: Platforms, Content Moderation, and the Hidden Decisions That Shape Social Media.* New Haven: Yale University Press, 2018.

Hern, Alex. "Revealed: Catastrophic Effects of Working as a Facebook Moderator." *Guardian,* September 17, 2019, https://www.theguardian.com/technology/

2019/sep/17/revealed-catastrophic-effects-working-facebook-moderator.

Hopkins, Nick, et al. "Facebook Files." *Guardian*, May 21–25, 2017, https://www.theguardian.com/news/series/facebook-files.

Newton, Casey. "The Trauma Floor: The Secret Lives of Facebook Moderators in America." *Verge*, February 25, 2019, https://www.theverge.com/2019/2/25/18229714/cognizant-facebook-content-moderator-interviews-trauma-working-conditions-arizona.

———. "The Terror Queue: These Moderators Help Keep Google and YouTube Free of Violent Extremism—and Now Some of Them Have PTSD." *Verge*, December 16, 2019, https://www.theverge.com/2019/12/16/21021005/google-youtube-moderators-ptsd-accenture-violent-disturbing-content-interviews-video.

Roberts, Sarah T. *Behind the Screen: Content Moderation in the Shadows of Social Media*. New Haven: Yale University Press, 2019.